The Fall

Colleen Nelson

GREAT PLAINS
TEEN FICTION

Copyright ©2013 Colleen Nelson

Great Plains Teen Fiction
(An imprint of Great Plains Publications)
345-955 Portage Avenue
Winnipeg, MB R3G 0P9
www.greatplains.mb.ca

All rights reserved. No part of this publication may be reproduced or transmitted in any form or in any means, or stored in a database and retrieval system, without the prior written permission of Great Plains Publications, or, in the case of photocopying or other reprographic copying, a license from Access Copyright (Canadian Copyright Licensing Agency), 1 Yonge Street, Suite 1900, Toronto, Ontario, Canada, M5E 1E5.

Great Plains Publications gratefully acknowledges the financial support provided for its publishing program by the Government of Canada through the Canada Book Fund; the Canada Council for the Arts; the Province of Manitoba through the Book Publishing Tax Credit and the Book Publisher Marketing Assistance Program; and the Manitoba Arts Council.

Design & Typography by Relish New Brand Experience
Printed in Canada by Friesens
Second Printing, 2013

Library and Archives Canada Cataloguing in Publication

Nelson, Colleen
    The fall / Colleen Nelson.

Issued also in electronic formats.

ISBN 978-1-926531-65-6
    I. Title.

PS8627.E555F34 2013   jC813'.6   C2012-908060-8

ENVIRONMENTAL BENEFITS STATEMENT

Great Plains Publications saved the following resources by printing the pages of this book on chlorine free paper made with 100% post-consumer waste.

TREES	WATER	ENERGY	SOLID WASTE	GREENHOUSE GASES
10 FULLY GROWN	4,533 GALLONS	4 MILLION BTUs	303 POUNDS	836 POUNDS

Environmental impact estimates were made using the Environmental Paper Network Paper Calculator 3.2. For more information visit www.papercalculator.org.

FSC
www.fsc.org
MIXTE
Papier issu
de sources
responsables
FSC® C016245

For my boys, James and Thomas

Monday

BEN

Shoving my skateboard into my locker, I grabbed my binder and raced to the computer lab. As I slunk into the spot Tessa had saved for me, Ms. Jimenez tapped her watch and raised an eyebrow. I was late, again.

"Hey," I said to Tessa, turning on the computer and waiting for it to hum to life.

"Hey." Tessa didn't look up as the keys clicked under her fingers. Two braids hung on either side of her face and she'd pushed a black knit cap so far off her head I wondered why she bothered wearing it.

"I nailed a 360 hard flip yesterday after you left."

She rolled her eyes at me. "I got your texts. All of them." She acted like she wasn't impressed, but Tessa would have texted me too if she'd landed a 360 hard flip.

"Come on, landing that trick is worth at least three texts," I whispered back.

"We're on Module B," she said watching me flip through the workbook. "Maybe a 360 *double* flip. Your 360 hard flip was only worth two, at most."

Ms. Jimenez stood in front of my computer. I wiped the smirk off my face and sat up straighter. "Ben, you didn't hand in yesterday's assignment. Do you have it?"

I groaned. "Can I hand it in tomorrow?"

"Tomorrow," she said with a warning tone, "or it's a zero, got it?"

"Got it."

According to my teachers, I'm a smart kid who needs to apply himself. According to my mom, I'm a smart kid who needs to spend less time skateboarding and more time studying. I'd be popular and on the honour roll if I put as much effort into making friends and doing homework as I do into nailing a new trick. But, I'd rather be sponsored than popular, and I'd rather be at the skatepark than the library.

The lunch bell rang and kids stampeded to the cafeteria.

I heard Cory Anderson and the Dumont brothers behind me. Like a freight train, they were hard to ignore. From the corner of my eye, I watched as they surrounded a guy a few lockers down. "Heard you got a new phone," Taz said, cracking his neck. The biggest of the three, he was built like a battering ram and used to play football. All muscle, he moved in close to the kid, trapping him.

"Mind if we take a look at it?" Cory, also a head taller than the scrawny tenth grader and smoother than Taz, reached behind the kid's head and grabbed it off the locker shelf. Turning the phone over in his hands, he glanced at the kid, who looked like he was going to cry. I didn't know the kid at the locker, but felt sick watching him lose his phone. They were toying with him. I wished they'd just take it and put him out of his misery.

Luke, Taz's younger brother, stepped back to look out for teachers. Softer and rounder than his brother, with a bristly thatch of brown hair, his eyes darted up and down the hallway. I wasn't quick enough to look away and he caught me watching. I opened my mouth to say something and then closed it when he smirked at me. There was nothing I could say to make them leave the kid alone. Better to just get my lunch and get the hell out of the hallway. Luke cleared his throat as a teacher turned the corner into the hallway. Taz and Cory moved away from the kid, and Cory slid the phone into his pocket.

The kid seethed helplessly as the teacher walked past—Cory, Taz and Luke's presence a threat against him saying anything. I could have told on them. The teacher was close enough for me to catch the scent of his cologne, but I stayed mute.

"Hey! Taz, look what I found," Cory exclaimed with fake surprise. "A phone!"

"Sure hope nothing bad happened to its owner. I heard some crazy shit's been going on, kids getting beaten up, things like that," Taz said. A menacing look distorted his face.

The kid shot a hateful look at Taz, but didn't say anything. Cory and the Dumont brothers backed away, waved at the boy and sauntered down the hallway as if they owned it. As they passed, Cory rammed Luke into me. He crushed me against the locker, squeezing the air out of my lungs and I dropped my lunch. Two cans of pop fell to the floor and Cory booted the orange down the stairs like a soccer ball. Luke staggered to get his balance while the other two kept walking.

Rubbing my shoulder, I bent down to pick up what was left of my lunch. A dime of weed lay on the floor. "Mr. Dumont!" A teacher bellowed behind me. Without thinking, I scooped up the bag and stuffed it in my pocket.

Why the hell had I picked it up? I didn't even smoke. If the teacher caught me, I'd get suspended, or worse. My heart started to hammer in my chest.

The teacher marched up the hallway towards Luke. "What's going on here?" He sounded pissed off already. With a flushed face, I backed up against the lockers.

"Nothing." Luke sneered at the teacher. "Talk to my brother. He's the one who pushed me."

"Get outside, Mr. Dumont. You're suspended from the cafeteria for the rest of the week."

Luke threw up his hands in disgust. "What about Taz? He pushed me!" The teacher walked away, ignoring Luke's shouts.

My fingers closed around the bag in my pocket. "Hey, uh, Luke?"

"What?" He looked like he wanted to punch me.

"You dropped something." Should I pass it to him now? In the hallway? The bag stuck to my clammy fingers.

Luke gave a relieved sigh. "Dude! I thought it was gone. I almost shit my pants when the teacher came over. Good thing you picked it up, huh?" He gave me a lopsided smile.

"Yeah, good thing." Pulling the dope out of my pocket, I slapped it on his palm and walked as quickly as possible down the stairs to the cafeteria.

"What took you so long?" Tessa asked when I found her sitting at our usual table.

"You know that kid in grade ten, a few lockers down from me? Skinny and he always wears that green hoodie."

Tessa shrugged.

"Well, he got his new phone stolen."

She unwrapped a granola bar and let the crinkly wrapper fall to the ground. "Who took it?"

"Cory Anderson, Taz and Luke Dumont."

"Did you say anything?"

I looked at her like she was crazy. "So they could come after me next?" I took a bite of the sandwich I'd saved from the floor and ignored her disapproving stare.

Tessa popped the lid on a can of ravioli. Everything Tessa eats comes from the inner aisles of the grocery store. I've never seen her eat a piece of fruit or drink anything that needed refrigeration. "Do you want to go downtown to skate tonight? We could take the bus and my dad could pick us up after his shift."

"Can't," I said. Gummy, white bread stuck to the roof of my mouth and it took my tongue a minute to wedge it out. "Jimbo is doing his fatherly duty tonight."

Tessa snorted. "Ten bucks says he doesn't show."

"Ten bucks he shows, but can't remember what grade I'm in."

"You should just bail. Why do you care so much about seeing him anyway?"

I shrugged. "He's my dad. I have to."

He left when I was seven. Mom had sat me down and given me the standard, it's-not-your-fault-Mom-and-Dad-still-love-you-we-just-can't-live-together-anymore speech. I believed her about the not living together part, but the rest of it I doubted. If he loved me so much wouldn't he want to see more than a few times a year? Mom kept promising that one day he'd realize what a great kid I was. Eight years later, and "one day" still hadn't come.

Tessa scoffed, and flung a braid over her shoulder. "You don't *have* to do anything. He's a deadbeat and he's never going to change." Tessa dove into her can of ravioli, the noodles hung limp and fleshy off the end of her plastic fork. "Never," she said with authority.

The Fall

I opened my mouth to argue. But, when she arched an eyebrow at me, I shut it.

The stairs at Gary B. Tucker High School are off-limits for skateboarding, but I was still waiting for Jim half an hour after school let out. I tried a few boardslides on the stair rails. And then a couple of huge ollies from the top of the stairs to the bottom. A few more tricks and Jim was officially forty-five minutes late.

It wasn't like I'd been looking forward to seeing him, but not having him show sucked. Had he forgotten? Or did he just not want to hang out? It's not like we had a lot in common. He tried to talk about hockey and baseball, but all I knew about was skateboarding. If he asked about my buddies at school, I stared at my shoes, unwilling to admit Tessa was the only person I hung out with. When he asked if I was raising any hell, I shrugged. Would he like me more if I were a troublemaker, with friends like Cory, Taz and Luke, instead of a skater?

At least Mom's taught me not to expect much from him, that way, when he does screw up, I can't get upset. The thing is: how much less could I expect from him? You'd think he'd be curious what I looked like after six months. Mom said I was growing like a weed and glared at me every time my toes started to push against a pair of shoes she'd bought me two months ago. Even though Mom never said anything, I could tell she saw my dad's face every time she looked at my blue eyes and bushy, blond eyebrows. The only resemblances to her were my thin-lipped mouth and perfectly straight teeth that had never needed braces. Good thing. We couldn't have afforded them anyway.

I texted Tessa. "I o u 10 bux, J's a no sho. Wanna go to sk8park?"

Right away my phone buzzed. "Ur dads a losr. B there in 20 min"

The skatepark was in a big, empty field across from the train tracks. It was built by the city to keep kids out of trouble, but half the time this was where the trouble was. A clump of bushes on one side was littered with empty beer and liquor bottles from bush parties and the corrugated metal siding on the old arena next door was covered with layers of tags. During the daytime, most of the kids who come here wanted to skate, but at night it became a hangout for anyone looking to get messed up.

Tessa was sitting on the far side of the bowl, dangling her feet off the edge and drawing something on her shoes. She waved at me as I sauntered across the field. There were a couple of other girls, who weren't skaters, hanging out today too, which sucked. It meant every guy would be trying stupid stuff to impress them.

I dropped my board in and cruised past the girls to land at Tessa's feet. "Your dad's a loser," she said without looking up.

"He probably forgot what school I went to."

Tessa squinted at me. "Aren't you mad?"

I shrugged, "Nah."

"Still. He should have come." She fixed me with one of her looks that dared me to argue and if I did, she already had an argument ready to shoot down whatever I said. "You must be a little pissed off?"

"I'm pissed that I waited so long," I said meeting her eyes, "I should have known he wasn't coming when he was five minutes late. I wished I'd left then."

"But, if he'd come and you hadn't been there, you'd feel guilty. That's why you waited. You didn't want to hurt his feelings." Tessa's always trying to toughen me up, make me stand up for myself. "You've got to tell him off, Ben. Let him know he can't treat you like crap." Tessa narrowed her eyes at me again. If I didn't give in, she'd never drop it and I wouldn't get to skate.

"Yeah, you're right."

With a satisfied smile, she capped the marker and slipped her shoes back on.

"How long have those girls been here?" I asked nodding in their direction.

Tessa shot them a disgusted look. "Since I got here." Jumping off the ledge, she landed beside me. "We should go to the new indoor skatepark this weekend. I saw pictures online and it looks sick." Her eyes, rimmed with thick black liner, shone with excitement.

I nodded. "Yeah. Sounds good. I heard Rox got some new decks in." Rox was the best skate store in the city. It was owned by a guy named Mitch who'd gone pro. His store carried all the best decks, trucks and gear. I fingered the worn edges of my board. "This one's toast."

I pulled my helmet and wrist guards out of my backpack. The helmet was old school, with a turquoise shell and orange chin-strap. My mom bought it on eBay for my fourteenth birthday. It's kind of dinged up after two years of abuse, but better the helmet than my head.

"You bringing it?" Tessa asked with a nod to the gear that I only wore when I really wanted to skate, not just goof around practicing tricks.

Grinning, I clicked the chinstrap buckle and kicked my board into my hands, ready to start my ride. "Oh yeah."

I dropped in and took the first lap slow, rolling with the momentum of the bowl. Gravel cracked under the wheels as I pushed off harder gaining speed. With a huge push, I propelled myself up the side and grabbed the board in mid-air with a hand-plant. A rush of air hit me when I nailed the landing and sailed around the bowl. My dad, the giggling girls and everything else melted away. The wheels felt like part of my body, like my feet didn't end at my toes, but had morphed into a skate deck and wheels. Nothing else existed, but me alone in the bowl ripping up each side and falling back to Earth.

At some point, though, I had to stop. Doing a perfect tre flip and kicking my board up into my hands, I looked toward Tessa. She wasn't even looking at me. I followed her gaze and saw Cory Anderson and Luke Dumont sitting with the girls. All of them stared back at me. My cheeks got hot.

Luke jumped in the bowl and walked towards me.

"You saved my ass today." Luke's sickly sweet pot smoke breath hit me in the face. "Can I pay you back?" His grin was open and friendly, like he'd just heard a great joke and wanted to share it with me.

I unbuckled my chinstrap and edged away. "No, I'm good."

"Yeah!" he laughed. "You got your own stash. Cool."

I didn't bother to correct him and moved towards Tessa.

He followed me. "What's your name?"

"Ben," I mumbled.

"Ben!" He held up his fist for a bump. "How long have you been riding?"

"A few years."

I glanced at Tessa who was watching us with narrowed eyes.

"Is that your girlfriend?" he asked.

"That's Tessa." As if her name should answer the question. She'd gone back to colouring her shoes, but kept flicking her eyes in my direction. The chemical smell of markers assaulted me, strong and heady.

"Cor, me and Taz are coming back here tomorrow night to party. You should come too."

I stared at Luke, speechless. Me hanging out with them was laughable, but Luke was serious. He stood waiting for me to say something. "Uh, maybe." I glanced at Tessa, hoping she couldn't hear us. I didn't want to explain about the pot and Luke's sudden interest in me. "Later," I said. He held his fist up again. I gave it a more enthusiastic bump and walked to the edge of the bowl.

Planting my palms on the concrete ledge, I pulled myself up; it seemed bizarre that the strong, sinewy forearms were mine. Before the winter, I'd been a skinny kid whose collarbone stuck out of t-shirts.

"What did he want?" Tessa asked, without taking a break from her sneaker artistry, which looked like a series of interwoven stars stacked on top of each other.

I shrugged. "Luke? He's just being friendly, I guess. Said he liked my ride."

Tessa scoffed and capped her marker. "Those guys are never just being friendly. They always want something."

"It *was* a sick ride."

"Whatever." Tessa leaned towards me, "They walk around school like they own it, especially Cory." She shot him a look across the bowl. Everyone at Tucker High had an opinion on the Dumont brothers and Cory Anderson. Tessa wasn't a fan; she thought they were assholes. But, Tessa thinks most people are assholes.

When I didn't say anything, she rolled her eyes and tossed my backpack to me. "Your mom called like a hundred times while you were in Benjiland." Benjiland is Tessa and Mom's nickname for what happens to me when I'm skating and forget the rest of the world exists.

"How'd you know it was Mom?" I asked, digging my phone out.

"I'm here and no one else ever calls you."

Mom had phoned a couple of times, probably to check up on Dad and make sure he showed.

"Hey, Mom. I'm at the skatepark and—"

"At the skatepark? Did you forget you were supposed to meet your dad?"

"He never showed. I'll be home in fifteen minutes." I clicked the phone shut before she could start a rant about Jim.

As Tessa and I started to walk back to the road, I heard Luke shout, "Hey!" I turned and he was sitting with one arm around a blond girl who had on a low-cut shirt and a nose ring. "Bring your girlfriend too, Dude! See you tomorrow!"

With a half-hearted wave, I heard Tessa snort beside me.

"I told him you weren't my girlfriend."

"It's not that," she said quietly. "Why does he want to hang out with you?"

"Because I'm super cool?" My suggestion was met with an eye roll.

"Hanging out with them is a bad idea."

We were a few meters away from the skatepark when I heard someone shouting. "Yo, Skaterboy!" I turned back. Cory had picked up a board and was poised at the top of bowl to start skating. He gave his half-smoked joint to one of the girls and held up his hands as if he was quieting a riotous concert crowd. "Watch this!" With a huge push off the side, he plunged down the bowl and popped up on the other side. A second later he disappeared and swooped down into the bowl and caught air on the other side a few feet from where the girls sat. One of them shrieked and covered her eyes as she fell into her friend's lap. The whole skatepark stopped to watch him.

I heard Tessa growl under her breath. "He's such a show-off."

She was right, he wasn't that good, but his power and recklessness made up for his lack of skill. It was like a car accident, I knew it would get ugly, but couldn't tear my eyes away.

The Fall

His ride came to a brutal end when he wiped out. I winced. It would hurt to sit down tomorrow. The whole skatepark whistled and clapped for him. When Cory stood up, he stared at me. "Come on back, Skaterboy. Show us what you got."

A queasiness rose in my stomach at his challenge.

"Go," Tessa hissed. "You're better than he is."

Shaking my head, I took a step backward as his audience turned to look at me. "I gotta go," I mumbled. Tessa gave a frustrated sigh and followed me.

"Boo!" Cory yelled at my back. "Boo!" The other kids joined in and I grit my teeth against the jeers.

"Why didn't you skate? You would have kicked his ass," Tessa said as we walked back to the main road.

Easy for her to say. Cory Anderson hadn't challenged her to anything. "I didn't feel like it." We walked in silence for while.

"You're going to call your dad, right?" Tessa asked. Her braids bumped rhythmically against her shoulders.

"My mom's probably going to lash into him pretty good for ditching me."

Tessa tilted her head at me, which meant she had more to say on the topic, whether I wanted to hear it or not. "It would be better if you told him yourself. He can't treat you that way and think he can get away with it."

"Whatever, Tessa. It's not a big deal."

"It is a big deal!" She was getting irritated and stopped walking to force me to give her my full attention. "Cory Anderson. Your dad. When are you going to learn not to be such a wuss?"

"I didn't feel like skating anymore," I said. "And my dad, you know what he's like. A puff of smoke that floats in and out of my life." I gave her a crooked smile hoping she'd believe that it didn't bug me. Tessa threw her arms up in exasperation and started walking. I grabbed the hat off her head and ran a few steps ahead, laughing as she swore at me. I taunted her that way until we got to the bus stop.

I could see Mom pacing in front of the living room window with the phone pressed to her ear. She was still wearing her nurse's aide uniform: a mint green button-up work shirt, matching pants and really ugly white shoes with rubber soles.

The lace curtain covering the small window in the door fluttered when I shut it behind me. She was talking to Dad; it was the only time her voice took on a shrill, angry tone. I tried to sneak down the hall to my room, but she grabbed the strap of my backpack and dragged me into the living room. "Here he is right now. You can apologize yourself." Her eyes blazed as she put the phone to my ear and crossed her arms.

"Hey," I said wishing I didn't have to do this right now. Or ever.

Dad sighed and I imagined him rubbing a hand through his thinning blond hair. "Aw, Ben. I'm sorry. I meant to be there. I pulled an all-nighter at work. Guess I missed my alarm." He waited for me to say something. Tessa's advice to tell him how I really felt came back to me.

"Ben? Are you there?"

"Yeah." I wanted to ask him, why wasn't he at the front door apologizing? Wasn't I worth a visit, even if it was for five minutes? Feeling the prickle of tears behind my eyes, I held the receiver tighter and waited for him to make another bullshit date to see me.

He forced a cheerful tone. "How about we try for next week?"

I took a deep breath before I chickened out. "Nah, don't worry about it. I'll call you ... sometime." Awkward pause. "Bye." Pressing the hang-up button, I tossed the phone on the couch.

Mom squeezed my shoulder. "You hungry?"

I shrugged.

She reached up to ruffle my hair. "I'll start dinner."

I went to my room, let my backpack fall to the floor and flopped onto my bed. He slept in, missed his alarm, and left me waiting at school for forty-five minutes. So, why did I feel like the jerk for hanging up on him? What was wrong with me? Burying my head in the pillow, I wished I didn't care if he showed up. But, I did care, and whatever I'd told Tessa about not caring was a lie.

The warm, spicy scent of chili powder drifted down the hallway to my room. Mom was cooking my favourite dinner: tacos. Meat sizzled and her knife banged as she chopped tomatoes. Normally, she would have called me to help her, but that's one thing about my mom, she knows when I just want to be alone.

TAZ

The sky was fading from pink into deep purple as Taz and Luke sat in the backyard on metal lounge chairs. Taz had chipped off the plastic armrests piece by piece, and the lawn around him, scrubby and bald in patches, was now littered with oddly shaped bits. Someone on the street was barbequing and the scent wafted over. He hadn't eaten dinner yet and his stomach growled.

Crunching his empty can and tossing it aside, he reached for a second beer. "To football!" he said holding it up.

Luke grinned. "To football. Fuck 'em!" He chugged the beer and belched.

Taz leaned back. He wished he could be more like Luke and not care so much. But that afternoon, as he'd stood in the parking lot after school watching Coach lecture the players, he'd felt regret. Senior year and he wasn't playing ball.

And it wasn't his fault. It was his dad's.

"Hey," Luke said. "We should light that thing." A rusty fire pit sat between their chairs; ashes and charred wood were piled inside. He dug in his pockets for a lighter. "What do we use for kindling?"

Taz looked around. A recycling box sat by the garage door stacked with newspapers and aluminum cans. "Give me your lighter." He held out his hand and Luke tossed it to him.

Taz rolled up a newspaper and lit the end like a torch. Moving closer to Luke, he waved it over the bottom of Luke's feet. "Piss off," Luke jumped out of the chair and tripped on what was left of their six-pack. Taz erupted with laughter and stepped closer to his brother with the torch, singeing the hem of his jeans. Luke banged his heel on the grass to put it out. "Get away from me!" Taz inched closer with the flame, like a wolf stalking its prey, as Luke crab-walked towards the fence.

Taz liked picking on Luke. It was his way of settling the score. Luke was the one their dad asked to go fishing and joked with at dinner. He was the one their mom talked with after work, who could make her laugh when she'd had a long day. Luke didn't know it, but Taz wished he'd been the one blessed with less will and more of his brother's goofball charm.

"I'm serious, man!" Luke laughed. "Stop trying to set me on fire! I'm gonna fart," he warned, "And make a natural gas explosion." In spite of himself, Taz laughed. He put the newspaper into the fire pit, where it burned itself out. Crumpling more sheets of newspaper into balls, he ripped tufts of dry grass out of the ground and sprinkled it on top.

"We gotta find something more to keep it going," he told Luke as he lit another torch, running the lighter's flame around the edge. He loved watching the paper turn black, curl on itself and then disappear.

"What about this?" Luke asked, grabbing a wooden bird feeder from its hook by the back door. He dumped out the seeds and pushed it inside the fire pit. The dying flames licked at the sides and then took hold, slowly creeping up to the roof and then engulfing it. The fire picked up momentum and Luke stuffed more newspapers in to keep it going, his face glowing with excitement. Neither of them spoke as they moved around the yard gathering things to stoke the fire; oven mitts, a straw wreath hanging on the door, a few dead branches snapped off a tree. "What do you think Dad would do if he caught us?" Luke asked.

"I don't know," Taz replied. A couple of years ago, he would have been able to predict his dad's behaviour, but not anymore.

Taz tested a fence board. White paint had peeled off exposing slivers of grayed, dry wood and rusty nails. Grabbing the top end, he yanked and it pulled away from the rickety fence, squeaking as the nails resisted his force. The wood was rough and brittle and cracked as he stomped on the middle to break it in half. Tossing the boards on, they grinned at each other over the fire.

"What about the garage? There'd be lots of stuff in there." Luke raised an eyebrow at Taz, daring him to bust the door open. This is how it was with them, each one pushing the other further.

"Move out of the way," Taz ordered and rammed his shoulder and hip against the door. After a few tries, the doorframe splintered and he was able to kick the door open. Taz scanned the shelves and saw a red, plastic container of gasoline. Holding it over his head, like a trophy, he whooped. "Hell yeah!"

"Oh, shit!" Luke laughed and raced outside to watch his brother. Taz trickled the gasoline onto the fire, suddenly aware of what he was doing and mesmerized by his own recklessness. It was too late now, the flame caught the chemical and in second, the air sucked past him and erupted into a bright orange flame. He was still holding the gasoline canister.

He heard Luke call his name, and as he turned, a blast caught him in the face. Cold pellets of water pierced his skin. Luke howled with laughter as he sprayed his brother and doused the fire. "You're a fucking asshole!" Taz shouted.

"Who saved your life! You were gonna blow yourself up holding the gas beside the fire. Blow up the whole fucking neighborhood too."

Taz tossed the open gasoline canister onto the ground and was about the wrestle the hose away from his brother when he heard sirens. "Shit! Let's get outta here."

Luke dropped the hose, still running, and followed his brother. "What about the beer?" Two of the six they'd brought sat on the grass.

"Leave it," Taz ordered, unlatching the gate and dashing off into the back lane. Luke ignored him and ran back. Taz swore under his breath. The sirens were getting closer and if a neighbour saw them, they'd be busted. Maybe a neighbour had already seen them and called it in. He doubled back and grabbed the hood of his brother's sweatshirt. "Come on!" Taz yelled as Luke stuffed the cans in the pouch of his hoodie.

From behind chain link fences dogs barked, egging them on, as they raced down the alley. Taz slowed down so Luke could catch up, his face was red with exertion, the beer cans bouncing in his pocket. Giving each other a high-five, they slowed to a trot, and then a walk as they turned onto their block. They'd retell this story, turning it into brotherly legend; laughing at each other and the mess they'd created in some stranger's back yard.

Tuesday

CORY

It had bothered Cory all night that the skater had walked away from him—as if Cory wasn't worth his time. The skater had made him look like a loser in front of the whole skatepark. And now, as he drove to school with Taz and Luke, he saw the kid rolling on his board to school. He probably passed him everyday without realizing it, but now the skater was on his radar. He smirked. Poor kid.

"Who's that kid? The skater?" Cory elbowed Luke and pointed.

Luke groaned and made a face as he tried to remember. "Ben, I think? He watched you take that kid's phone yesterday. Didn't say anything, either. Found my weed too, when I dropped it."

"And gave it back?" Taz gave Luke a look of disbelief, almost rear-ending the car in front of him. The truck jerked forward as he slammed on the brakes, Cory slapped his hand on the dash.

"You're a shitty driver, dude." Cory clenched his jaw. His scar throbbed. No one said anything and the mood in the truck darkened. "What's his deal?" He gave a chin nod to Ben. As they sat at the stoplight, he caught up to them and kicked the skateboard into his hands, waiting for the light to change.

Luke turned to look, but Taz kept his eyes on traffic in front of him. "I don't know. Thought it was cool he helped me out." Cory squinted at Ben as they pulled ahead of him. "He tore up the bowl yesterday."

"You pissed that he didn't come back when you started skating?" Taz asked. They'd known each other since elementary school. Two kids kicked out of the class, they'd forged a friendship in the hallway and then on the playground; natural athletes it was the two of them playing against the whole class. Sometimes Luke would join in, but he never had the same hunger to compete as Cory and Taz. Even as kids, they knew they had to be on the same team or they'd destroy each other in their desire to win.

Cory smirked. "He's a nobody."

"A nobody who walked away from you. You losing your edge?" Taz snickered.

Cory wound up and punched Luke in the gut, who coughed and sputtered in surprise. "What the hell? Why'd you do that?" He moaned.

"Couldn't reach Taz." A slow grin stretched over Cory's face.

Taz laughed as he drove, ignoring his brother. "You're such an asshole!"

"We gonna party tonight?"

"Yeah. Bush party at the skatepark." A wooded area between the park and the road had a clearing in the middle. Bright lights around the park, a safety precaution, lit the bushes up just enough to make it the perfect spot for kids to congregate in the night.

"Maybe we should invite the skater. School him a bit." Cory made the comment off-handedly, but the idea began to take shape in his head. There was something appealing about deflowering the skater, bringing him over to the dark side and finding out if he'd walked away because he was stupid, or had balls bigger than most kids at Tucker High.

Taz pulled up to the school. Kira was leaning against the railing waiting for Cory and talking with some other girls. When he got out of the truck, she smiled at him, tossing her hair over her shoulder. He watched a few guys shoot jealous looks at him for scoring the hottest girl in school. She was a year younger, the same age as Luke, but he didn't care. Every guy wanted her and that was what mattered.

"Hey," he said and sidled up to her, slipping an arm around her waist. She smelled like vanilla and coconut, sweet and tropical. "Bush party tonight, you coming?"

She gave him one of her looks, long and full of meaning. "I have a test tomorrow. I can't party."

He took his arm away. "Okay, nerd."

Kira rolled her eyes and turned to her friends. Bored with the conversation, he jumped over the railing and went to find Taz and Luke.

They'd bummed smokes and were hanging out around the corner. The ground around them was covered with the butts of a winter's worth of cigarettes. The kid they were standing with offered one to Cory before he even had to ask. As the lighter's flame flared, Cory took a deep breath, enjoying the buzz of nicotine racing into his system.

Cory looked out across the school field, its grass matted and brown, to the goal posts. "You gonna play ball this year?" he asked Taz.

Taz shot him a look. "After last year? No."

"They won't let you?"

"Can't even *watch* a game. I'm banned for life."

Cory hadn't been there when it had happened, but he'd heard how Taz had gone into a rage, attacking his dad with a helmet.

Taz never talked about it, but Cory wasn't surprised; Mr. Dumont wasn't winning any Father of the Year contests.

Luke finished his cigarette and tossed it on the ground. "Did you ask Cory about working this summer?"

Taz shook his head. "Not yet. What d'you think?" he turned to Cory. Last summer, when Taz had started a lawn care business, he'd asked Cory to work with him. But, Cory had turned him down and taken a job doing construction with his uncle. It had paid well, but the other guys were assholes who didn't want the boss's nephew hanging around.

"Just you, me and Luke?" Cory asked.

"Maybe one more if we got busy enough. You know Russ, the guy who owns the window washing business? We partied with him a few times," he said. "Thought we could ask him to recommend us to his customers. Kind of promote us."

Taz was always thinking of ways to make money. Cory didn't care about that. He could steal a bit from him mom or sell something. When he needed money, he found a way. But they would be graduates this summer. It was time to make some serious coin and think about moving out. Hanging out with his buddies all summer and mowing grass sounded better than running errands at a site.

Cory took a final drag on his cigarette and stared at Kira. Her long, dark hair waved behind her in the wind. She'd be working too, saving up for university. "Yeah, why not?" he tossed the butt onto the ground where it smoldered, a thin trail of smoke rising up.

Luke grinned at him. "Wicked, dude!"

Cory narrowed his eyes at Luke, whose smile faded. "God, you're more excited about me cutting grass than you are about getting laid." Cory watched with satisfaction when Luke's cheeks turned pink.

The bell rang and a collective groan sounded as kids drew one last, long puff of their cigarettes and dragged themselves inside the school. Cory waited until everyone else had gone inside and took a deep breath, the smell of cigarettes lingered in the air. Had anyone realized he hadn't gone inside? Kira? Taz? Luke? Had anyone cared?

Spitting the bitter taste of nicotine out of his mouth, he directed a foamy wad at the door. Bubbles of saliva dribbled down the metal to the cement. He didn't care if no one had seen, it made him feel better.

BEN

Tessa had to babysit the next day after school, so I went to the skatepark by myself. I strapped on my helmet and pads and was about to take my first ride when Luke, Taz and Cory pulled up in a green pick-up truck. The sides were pockmarked with rust and it coughed and sputtered like a smoker who'd run ten blocks.

When the three of them spilled out of the truck, the energy of the skatepark changed. Girls started to laugh more loudly and guys clustered in larger groups and acted like they'd just had a shot of testosterone. Luke raised a hand in my direction. I gave him a chin nod and dropped my board in. The wheels grated against the concrete as I took a few easy rides on each side of the bowl and then built up some speed and did a buttery 5-0 to fakie on the coping. As I went past Luke, Taz and Cory, an overdose of cheap, spicy cologne hit me and I heard them cheer for me.

I pumped around the bowl aiming to fly over the back-to-back quarter pipes. With one final push, I aired over the spine and grabbed the edge of my board. I'd seen the trick in skate videos, but it was the first time I'd tried it. The rough grit of the griptape scratched my fingers as the board almost shot out from under me when I landed. I wobbled, but didn't wipe out. Even Tessa would have been impressed.

Cory crouched on the edge above me. In the late afternoon sunlight, the pale, pink scar that scissored down his temple was more obvious. "Shit, dude. Where did you learn to ride?" After yesterday, his sudden friendliness made me uneasy.

Shrugging, I unsnapped the chinstrap so it hung loose around my neck. A fringe of hair fell over my eyes.

"That trick you did was sick. Are you sponsored?" Cory asked. His eyes reminded me of a German Shepherd's, with an amber centre with a dark ring around the outside. One minute they looked soft, but could turn hard the next.

"Nah," I shook my head and pulled myself out of the bowl.

"You should get a camera and shoot some footage, maybe put it on YouTube, or something." As Cory talked to me, Taz and Luke wandered over.

"What's this? The kid wants to go on YouTube?" Taz eyed me up and down and turned to Cory. Being called "kid" set my teeth on edge. "He might get sponsored if someone saw him," he said, as if he was an expert.

Luke nodded to his brother. "Yeah, he's good enough."

Putting a video on YouTube was a solid idea. Pop stars, rappers, comedians, lots of people were getting contracts from being spotted on the website. All you had to do was tape yourself and upload it onto the free website and millions of people could access it. If I had a decent video camera, I would have already done it.

Cory squinted at me like he was deciding something. "I'll take my mom's camera. We could do it this weekend." A train rumbled past on the tracks making it almost impossible to hear each other without shouting. A long whistle pierced the air.

"You ever post anything on YouTube before?" Taz asked Cory.

"Uh-huh. Remember, the video of us surfing the roof of your car on the highway? I posted that." He cracked his knuckles and gave Taz a sly grin.

Taz emitted a deep, throaty laugh. "Oh yeah? I got in so much shit for that! I didn't know that was you, you bastard!"

Taz threw a punch at Cory. It wasn't meant to hurt him, but Taz was built like a battering ram and any punch he threw was going to leave a mark. Luke laughed and egged them on as Cory landed a punch in Taz's gut making him stumble and gasp.

I started to back away. If they treated their friends like this, what were they like with their enemies? The fight came to an abrupt end when they grabbed the back of each other's neck in a headlock and then burst apart. "I beat up that Miller kid because I thought he did it!" Taz started laughing again, but winced and held his stomach.

"Yeah, I never liked that kid." The two of them started laughing again.

Luke caught my eye and grinned. I didn't smile back. I remembered seeing Tim Miller at school after he'd been beat up. His nose had swollen to double its size and both eyes had been ringed with purple bruises. A teacher had mumbled, "If you sleep with dogs, you'll get fleas," as he limped past.

"You going to party with us tonight?" Luke asked me.

"Maybe," I shrugged, hoping he'd drop it.

Cory leaned in close, forcing me to meet his eyes. "Thanks for grabbing Luke's shit the other day. We owe you one."

"Who do you hang with, anyway?" Taz asked.

"Uh, hang with? Like friends?"

Taz raised his eyebrows, a suspicious smirk on his face.

"Other skaters I guess. Tessa." The list was short. Too short.

"You should hang with us sometime," Cory offered. "We'd look after you." A grin spread over his face, but didn't reach his eyes.

"I gotta go." I stuffed my helmet in my backpack and hiked it up on my shoulder. Cory held out his hand for me to grab and then gave me a one-arm hug, patting my backpack. Caught off-guard, I saw other kids watching us, looking as surprised as I was. Taz moved over and gave me a pound-hug too, as if we were old friends. Confused, I turned to Luke. He'd edged closer to me.

"Can I chill at your place for while?" he asked in a low voice. Taz and Cory had already started to walk away without waiting for Luke. I guess that's how it works when you're the little brother.

"Yeah ... I guess." The words couldn't have sounded less sure.

Luke's goofy grin reappeared. He looked relieved. "I'm going with Benny. Catch you guys later," he shouted after them. They didn't even turn around.

Tessa picked that moment to text me. "whr r u?"

She'd be pissed if she knew I was hanging with Luke. I stuffed the phone back in my pocket, without replying.

Mom flashed a megawatt smile at me when I walked in with a friend from school who wasn't Tessa. Mom loves Tessa, but since—according to her—I'm starved for male companionship, she thinks the last thing I need is a best friend who's a girl. She put the pizza she was going to cook back in the freezer and pulled out some hamburgers instead. The backdoor slammed behind her as she went to light the barbeque.

I showed Luke my room. A collage of famous skateboarders, skateboards, decals I'd like to get for my skateboard, guys nailing tricks or aerial jumps and still shots of skateparks around the world papered the fake wood paneling. One of the ceiling tiles had fallen out, but I'd taped some pictures to cover the hole. Besides the pictures, my room was pretty plain: a single bed with a mattress that squeaked every time I turned over and crazy orange curtains that my mom had stapled over the window. On a sunny day the room glows like it's on fire. There was also a dresser with a round mirror, but most of my clothes lay heaped over a chair in the corner. Finding socks and underwear in the morning usually meant sorting through a pile of clean and not-so-clean clothes at the end of the bed and doing a sniff test.

Luke spent some time squinting at photos Mom had stuck around my mirror. He tapped one of me and my dad and laughed. It had been taken when I was about seven in front of the go-carts at an amusement park, just before my dad had moved out. My hair shone white in the sun and a gaping hole showed in my mouth from the two teeth I'd lost. Dad had a cigarette dangling from one side of his mouth. I remembered the smell of the cigarette on his hand as he'd laid it on my shoulder.

"Hey! I used to go here too with my dad!" Luke said pointing at the photo. "One time, we were playing arcades and I won the biggest prize, a stuffed blue dolphin. It was as big as me but I carried it the whole day. Taz was so pissed off that he didn't win anything. I think it's the only time I ever beat him at anything."

Mom knocked on the door and poked her head in. "Dinner's ready." The smell of charcoal and grilling meat would have drawn us out of my room anyway. She'd set up a folding patio table outside with a red vinyl tablecloth. The mustard, relish and ketchup were arranged on a tray in the center and we each had cutlery and a paper napkin stuck in a glass at our place. As Mom dished out the salad, the neighbor's dog started to bark at a squirrel running across the fence. The dog was tethered to a pole in the center of the yard and the chain clanged against the metal as he dashed to the end of his chain again and again.

We didn't live in the richest neighborhood. Small, white-stucco houses with chain link fences lined the street. Some had sagging roofs covered in moss and others had front steps falling away from the house, but everyone mowed their lawn, planted flowers in the summer and waved hello. As Mom said, when no one has anything, you all have something.

Luke inhaled his hamburgers and when Mom asked if he wanted another one, he smiled at her with bits of green relish stuck in his teeth and nodded. Mom laughed and shook her head, "Only a sixteen-year old boy could put away three hamburgers in one sitting," she said as she got up to put on one more. I'm no lightweight either when it comes to eating these days, but after two hamburgers and a plate of salad, I was done. I let out a huge belch. Luke high-fived me, and Mom gave me a look.

Fat dripped off the hamburger, hissing as it fell onto the charcoal and igniting a flame. Mom flipped the burger like a pro. "Do you have any brothers or sisters, Luke?"

"I have an older brother. He goes to Fuc—I mean, Tucker High too."

"And what about your parents?"

I groaned inwardly and shrank back in my chair a bit. Luke didn't seem to care, especially when she put the third hamburger in front of him with cheese dripping down the sides.

Between mouthfuls, Luke told her, "Mom works at Supervalue and my dad works construction and shi—I mean stuff."

I could tell by Mom's smile that she liked that Luke's parents were still married, as if it guaranteed he had a happy home.

Ketchup plopped on the plate as Luke stuffed the last bite into his mouth. He slouched back in his chair and put his hands behind his head. "Thanks, Ben's mom."

"You can call me Mrs. Olniuk," she said grinning at him.

"Where's Mr. Olniuk?" Luke asked casually. Immediately, Mom stiffened and cleared her throat.

"He lives in the West End," I jumped in with, "but I don't see him much. You know…" A breeze lifted the corners of the plastic tablecloth. Without hamburgers to hold them down, the paper plates almost blew off. Mom and I lunged for our plates, but Luke's arms didn't budge from behind his head.

"How come you don't see him much?"

I stared at Luke. He's barely talked to me my whole life and after a few burgers he wants my life story? "Cuz … he works a lot."

Luke snorted and tipped his chair so the two back legs wobbled under his weight. "My dad's not around much either. Even when he is, he isn't, you know?"

Mom reached across the table to take away our plates, her lips in a thin line. I knew what she was thinking, "Another dad who isn't there for his kid."

"What time is Taz picking you up?" I asked. The sun had set and goosebumps rose on my arms.

Luke let his chair drop and reached into his pocket for his cell. The phone had duct tape holding it together and he had to squint at the screen to make out the text. "He'll be here in an hour."

If it had been Tessa and I hanging out, we would have checked out the computer for some new tricks or flipped through some skateboard magazines. Sometimes we'd each take one end of the couch and watch TV. I didn't know what to do with Luke. Mom was right. I did need to hang out with guys more.

"He and Cory are a few blocks away at Kira Grayeye's house. Wanna walk over there?" Luke asked.

"Sure," I said, relieved to have something to do with him. A car down the street backfired as the gate clanged shut. Luke picked up a long, smooth stick and ran it along the fence. I followed a step behind, my skate shoes clomping through piles of slimy brown leaves dotting the sidewalk. When we got to the corner, Luke jabbed the stick into the ground like he was impaling something.

"You're going to hang out with us tonight, right?" Luke asked as we waited to cross the street. The pavement had cracked and shifted over the winter. Unsuspecting cars landed in a deep pothole in front of us. One totally bottomed out and Luke whooped in mockery. I snickered a little too.

Shrugging, I shook my head. "Not really my thing."

His laugh sounded like a bark. "You're full of shit."

Turning a corner, I spotted Taz's truck half way down the block. Luke picked up a rock and aimed at the truck, but it missed by a few feet and bounced in the middle of the street. "Let's go to the new Adam Sandler movie tomorrow night, okay?"

Before I could answer him, Cory and Taz clambered out of a house and bounded across the street to Taz's truck.

"So, you in? For the movie?"

I'd already promised Tessa I'd go with her, but Luke looked at me like I was about to grant him a dying wish. "Yeah, sure." Maybe Tessa could come with us? She'd see Luke wasn't such a bad guy, especially when his brother and Cory weren't around.

His face split in a grin. "Cool. Let's meet at the skatepark after school." He bellowed, "Yo!" and jogged to the truck as Taz fired up the engine.

I was almost on my block when the truck roared down the street. Taz lay on the horn.

The Fall

"Wimp-ass! See you tomorrow!" He hollered through the open window and flashed me the finger. Were they going to the movie too? "Great," I muttered under my breath, and kicked a rock across the pavement. There was no way Tessa would go now.

An old lady in her front yard wearing a housecoat and hair net straightened up and pursed her lips at me, as if I was the one who'd honked and yelled. I thought of Tim Miller and his cracked ribs. If you lie with dogs, you'll get fleas.

When I came home, a yellow sticky-note on the fridge said "Call Mama Pal."

The Paladopoulos' owned Plate-o's, a Greek restaurant that Mom worked at until last year when she got full-time work as a nurse's aide. When I was a baby, she used to bring me to her shifts and set up a playpen in the kitchen. Mama and Papa Pal are like grandparents. Since Mom's parents live in B.C. and I've never met Dad's, they are the only family we've got.

"Mom?" I called from the kitchen. "What does Mama Pal want?" She was sitting at the dining room table with papers and her cheque book spread in front of her. Never a good time to come home. Rubbing the pencil eraser against her temple, she barely looked up at me.

"She didn't say. There were two 411 charges on your cell bill last month." She waited for an explanation, or at least an apology. The cell phone had been a birthday present. But it wasn't much of a present when each month I had to answer for every penny I went over.

"Uh, yeah. Sorry. How much was it?"

Mom cleared her throat, which meant she was gearing up for a lecture.

Before she could start, I said, "Probably like four bucks, right? Add it to my tab," I grinned at her. But felt guilty when her shoulders slumped in futility.

"I hope Mama Pal has a job for you because that cell is going to get cut off if you don't stop—"

I'd already walked back into the kitchen and picked up the phone. The dial tone drowned out Mom's voice.

"Allo?" Mama Pal's thickly accented voice answered.

"Hey, Mama Pal, it's Ben." Sitting down, I also hoped she had a job for me. Whenever they had a big delivery arriving or had an especially disgusting job, like cleaning the meat freezer, they'd call me. They knew I wouldn't say no … or couldn't say no.

"Ah, Benny! I have job for you. I want new covers for chairs. You have gun for staples?"

I smiled. "Yeah, Mama, I have a staple gun."

There was a clatter in the background, like someone had dropped a tray of dishes and Mama Pal swore in Greek. "Aiiii! Fingers like an elephant!" All four feet, ten inches of Mama Pal could be as intimidating as a six foot five inch linebacker. "Okay, you come Sunday and work with Papa. Mama make souvlaki, just for Benny." I could almost taste the spicy pork dripping with oil. "Tell Patti 'hallo,' okay?"

"Okay, bye, Mama." Before I hung up the phone I could hear her berating the dishwasher for his clumsiness.

"What did Mama want?" Mom called from the dining room.

"They need me to work on Sunday," I called as I opened the fridge. My voice echoed in its emptiness, but now wasn't the time to point that out to Mom. A jug of juice sat at the back. Orange sludge had settled on the bottom. Shaking the container I poured myself a glass and gulped it down before I could really taste it.

The Fall

Mom was staring out the window, the bills and papers strewn around her, when I walked back into the dining room.

"Mom?"

She jumped when I said her name.

"Are you okay?" My throat burned from the acidic aftertaste of the juice.

"Uh, yeah," she said, shuffling some papers to one side of the table. "Ben, have you worked on your resume yet? You need to get going on that summer job."

"What about at the restaurant? Mama Pal said I could wash dishes." It was only April. Why was Mom already stressing about it?

Mom shook her head and rubbed her forehead. "Mama Pal already has a full-time dishwasher. She'll only be able to give you a few nights a week. Anyhow, I'm going to ask her if I can pick up a couple of shifts serving."

The orange juice rose up into my throat, its sour taste stinging. "Why?" Mom already worked as many shifts as the hospital could give her.

Letting her hands fall to the table, she looked defeated. "Because we need more money, that's why." Frustration seeped into her voice. "The car is on its last legs and our furnace probably needs to be replaced this winter. My savings are wiped out and by the end of the month, I barely have enough left to buy groceries."

"You mean its last wheels."

She gave me a confused look, "What?"

I grinned, "The car, you said legs, but it would be on its last wheels."

Mom slammed her fist on the pile of papers. "Shit, Ben! You think this is funny? I work forty hours a week or more to keep a roof over our heads and you're making jokes?" As quickly as her anger came, it left and she collapsed in her chair, hiding her face with her hands.

I froze in the middle of the room, not sure what to do. Mom raised her head and rubbed her forehead. "It would really help if you could look for a summer job. You're old enough to help out."

"Yeah, sure." I hung my head and walked to my room, closing the door quietly. Working a full time job would leave no time for skating. How would I get sponsored if I couldn't skate? Stuffing my pillow up under my chin, I picked at a piece of loose wallboard until a chunk came off in my hand. It wasn't fair that I had to pick up the slack because my dad was a deadbeat. Mom worked her ass off for us and Jim didn't do a thing.

"Ben?" Mom knocked and poked her head in. She sat on the edge of my bed and rubbed my back. "I didn't mean to take it out on you." She sighed.

Bunching the pillow behind my back, I sat up. "I can get a job. It's no big deal." Most of Mom's brown hair had fallen out of the clip she always wore and hung on both sides of her face. She'd been really pretty when she was young, with long, thick hair and skin that looked like she'd just washed her face. She was still pretty, in a Mom kind of way, but now she had a crease dug deep between her eyes and wiry gray hairs streaked through the brown.

Her eyes roamed my room. "It's not that. You don't need to know about the other stuff ... about the car and the furnace. That's for me to worry about." She laid her hand on my shin and gave it a gentle squeeze. "But, it would help if you would stop growing for two minutes," she said with a wry smile, "because if I have to buy you one more pair of shoes, I'm going to cripple your feet." She opened her arms for a hug.

I rolled my eyes to the ceiling. "Are you serious?"

With her arms still stretched in front of her like a zombie, she nodded her head. "Yes. Come here."

I fell into her hug and let her squeeze and pat my back until her maternal affection quota had been filled.

LUKE

Luke kept burping burger. He'd eaten too much at Ben's house and salty, greasy belches erupted from his stomach. Squished between Cory and Taz, yet again, he wished he hadn't been in such a rush to leave Ben's house. He liked Ben and he liked how Ben's mom had made them dinner and talked to them. His mom acted like she was afraid of his friends, retreating to the kitchen the second they walked in the house. Maybe it wasn't an act. Maybe she was scared.

Cory purposefully took up space in the truck, forcing him to sit on the hump between the driver and passenger side and giving Cory lots of room to rest his arm on the window. He's learned not to make a big deal out of things like that, it just made Cory more intent on finding ways to annoy him. Sometimes Taz came to his defense, but most of the time he laughed as Cory used him as a punching bag, or punch line.

"Is he gonna party tonight?" Cory asked as Taz started the engine.

Luke shrugged. "Nah, but we might go to a movie tomorrow."

"Good." Cory nodded and leaned over to look at Taz. "I love it when a plan comes together."

"What are you talking about? What plan?"

"Let the grown-ups talk," Cory said and leaned back with a satisfied grin on his face. Luke narrowed his eyes at Cory. Why did he have to be such an asshole?

Taz leaned on the horn, yelling out the window as they drove past Ben. Luke watched as Ben jumped at the noise, his face a mixture of surprise and annoyance. Keeping him in sight in the rearview mirror, Luke felt like a traitor, as if he should warn Ben, but he didn't know what to warn him about.

Ever since Taz had got kicked off the football team, there was a recklessness that hadn't been there before. Even at home. He made comments to his dad, trying to provoke him. Luke wished he could let it go. The fight at the field had been both their faults. His dad never should have shown up drunk and acted like an ass, but Taz had hit first, and then kept hitting.

"Where are we going?" he asked, looking to his brother.

"Pick up some beers and then head over to the skatepark." Taz glanced at Cory. "You got any cash?"

Cory shook his head. "No, but I got this." He dug a shiny new iPod out of his pocket. "I found it," he smirked, "on some kid at the bus stop and told him I'd beat his head in if he didn't give it to me."

Taz laughed and reached over to give Cory a fist bump. "You wanna pawn it? The place downtown is open til nine."

Luke settled in between his brother and Cory. There was a peace in not having to be the decision maker. Luke went with the flow and reaped the rewards: beer, smokes, weed. A lot of guys would have died for the set-up he had. Even Ben. Once he hung out with them, Ben would realize what he'd been missing.

Wednesday

BEN

"Are you serious, Ben?" Tessa asked with her hands on her hips, glowering at me through black eye make-up.

I shook my head innocently, "What?"

"You are going to hang out with the Dumont brothers and Cory Anderson?" The way she said it sounded like I was joining a gang of America's Most Wanted. Luke had texted me while we stood by our lockers and Tessa, who never misses anything, peeked at the message. "Sk8park 2nite then movie. Taz sez he'll drive. Cory's comin too."

"I didn't know Cory and Taz were going. I thought it was just Luke."

"Hello? Ben? You are like," she took a deep breath trying to find the words, "a chew toy to those pit bulls. They're going to eat you alive."

I slammed my locker shut with a metallic clang and wished Tessa would drop it. "I can take care of myself."

Tessa scoffed, her eyes narrowed and angry. "Since when?" She spun on her heel, a braid almost whacking me in the eye, and stalked off. I walked to class.

I sat in class fuming about Tessa's attitude. I didn't need another mom, I wanted a friend. She acted like she knew what was best for me, telling me how to deal with my dad and who I could be friends with. Hanging out with guys grew more appealing as I thought about all Tessa's flaws.

After school, I pushed open the front doors and saw Taz's truck idling in front of the steps. Luke was nodding his head to music pounding from the stereo. Swearing under my breath, I spun on my heel to sneak out the back doors. The truck, the music, the dope—it wasn't my scene. Tessa was right, I didn't belong with them.

My stomach dropped when Taz spotted me. He grabbed my shoulder like I was a kid in trouble and propelled me through the doors. "I was looking for you. Let's go."

Luke jumped out so I could sit in the middle. The radio blared and Taz put the truck into gear and it roared to life, rumbling like an oncoming train. Resting his arm on the back of the seat, Taz reversed out of the lot.

I fiddled with the trucks on my deck and spun the wheels, banging them to a stop with my palm. Excuses ran through my head: I had to work at the restaurant; my mom needed me at home; homework? But every time I was about to open my mouth, Luke grinned at me like I'd made his day. I didn't have the guts to bail on him. Just like I didn't have the guts to tell off my dad, or skate against Cory. With a heavy feeling in my stomach, I sat back. There was no getting out of this.

"Hey, Taz, tell Benny how you got the truck," Luke said over the music. Wedged between the brothers, when the truck hit a pothole, I rammed against them like a pinball. Its shocks were in the same condition as its paint job.

Taz didn't answer right away, so I stared uncomfortably out the windshield. My eyes watered from the dust and smell of pot inside the truck. Finally, in a deep voice that matched the rumble of the engine he told me, "I stole it."

I stared at him.

"Ha! Just screwing with you, man!" He thumped me on the arm, hard, and laughed. I fought the temptation to rub the spot he'd hit. His joke had loosened the tension though, and I relaxed into the seat. "I bought it last year when I started doing people's lawns, like mowing and shit. The money was pretty good. I'm doing it again this summer, but I'm going to hire some guys and advertise and then shovel snow in the winter. By next year, I'm going to trade in this piece of junk for a Mustang."

He must have made some serious cash if he could afford the truck and the gas for it. "Cool." I didn't know many kids who were able to afford their own ride at seventeen.

"I'm gonna work with Taz this summer, right Taz?" Luke asked, sticking his head out the window like a dog.

Taz nodded. "I'll need a few other guys too. Interested?" He shifted his glance to me.

"Uh, yeah." I tried to keep the enthusiasm out of my voice. "My mom was ragging on me about getting a job this summer." Maybe Tessa was wrong and Taz wasn't such a bad guy. I liked the idea of working outside and eating lunch on the tailgate of his truck in the sunshine. It would also leave time to skate.

We rolled up to the skatepark. A few kids hung out on the edges and a couple of BMX bikers stood on the rim ready to dive into the bowl. The only person actually skating had braids and a black board with a neon pink skull and crossbones on it.

"Hey, that's your girl. The bitchy one," Luke said pointing at Tessa.

"Yeah," I mumbled, not bothering to correct him.

A sly smile crept across Taz's face. He had a long mouth, but thin lips. He looked like a grinning jack-o-lantern when he smiled. "Let's go say hello!" He grabbed my head and rubbed the top of it with his knuckles. It hurt. I tried to yank my head away, but his arms were as thick as Duraflame logs.

Taz and Luke opened their doors and slid out of the truck. I swallowed hard. What was Tessa going to do when she saw me with them?

With her shoulders hunched around her ears and her head down, her lines stayed fluid, even as she swooped around the bowl and landed a sweet pop shove-it. Riding her board to the top of the bowl where it leveled out into a sidewalk, she grabbed her backpack. Without looking my way, she slipped it on and walked away, banging her board against her knee.

"Hey," Taz bellowed from across the bowl, "Where are you going? We brought your boyfriend!"

She didn't turn around.

My cell buzzed with a text. "u r an ass." Blinked up from Tessa.

"Shit," I whispered under my breath. I felt like someone had kicked me in the balls.

"You gonna ride?" Luke asked me. He wore his typical expectant smile. I didn't really feel like riding, but felt less like standing with him and Taz. Kids cleared out of the bowl when they saw me waiting on the side with my board. Looking around, I saw a few of them point me out to friends, as if I was somebody to watch, or maybe because of who I'd arrived with.

"Yeah, I guess." I didn't bother to put on my pads and dropped my board in. I rode the bowl without getting air or trying a trick. Benjiland. The rhythmic circles and roll of wheels on concrete drowned out the noise around me. I blocked out Taz and Luke's taunts and the pounding beat of someone's car stereo and focused on keeping the rhythm even and smooth. Up and down I rode, making waves around the bowl until my legs started to ache with the monotony.

"That was lame," Taz said when I kicked my board into my hands in front of him. I shrugged apologetically, but he'd already turned away from me.

A train's whistle screeched in the distance.

"Hey, Luke." The corners of Taz's lips curled as he grabbed his brother's sleeve forcing Luke to face him. "I bet you can't run across the tracks three times before that train comes." The words had barely left Taz's mouth before Luke was tightening his laces.

"Twenty bucks and I get to take your truck tonight," Luke said.

Taz took a quick look at the approaching train and then his brother. "Done."

"Dude," I stared in shock as Luke sprinted towards the tracks, "seriously?" Only Taz heard me, my voice drowned out by another piercing train blast.

It hadn't rounded the bend yet, but Luke had a field of flattened, dead grass to cross. His loping run took him past the thicket of trees and almost up the hill in front of the tracks. He stumbled once and used his hands to push himself upright.

Taz snorted. "He'll never make it." He sounded gleeful at watching his brother fail.

"Then why'd you make the stupid bet with him," I mumbled.

"Cuz that's who he is. The guy who'll do it. He always takes the bet." Taz narrowed his eyes, all his energy focused on Luke.

But you're his big brother, I wanted to say. You're supposed to look out for him.

Luke made it over the hill. The train whistled again and like approaching thunder, I felt the ground tremble. Luke made one pass and landed on the other side. The train rumbled into view.

Other kids in the skatepark crept closer, peering over each other to see who was racing the train. My lungs wanted to explode with air I hadn't exhaled. Luke raced across one more time. The train wasn't slowing down. It barreled ahead and blasted its whistle. The entire crowd of kids was silent as Luke ran over the tracks and then went down. I couldn't tell if he was on the tracks or had made it across.

Taz broke into a run. His body moved differently than Luke's. He didn't stumble up the hill, but took it in three strides, his bulk moving effortlessly. I'd dropped my board and raced behind him, pumping my arms and legs hard. We crested the hill at the same time. In flashes between the train's wheels I saw Luke lying face down on the other side. Leaves and bits of debris whipped around us, but as soon as the last car passed the trees, they stood motionless and the dust settled. It was silent, except for muffled laughter. Luke raised his fists in the air.

"Yaaaaaaaahhhhh!" The sound exploded from his belly and ripped through his vocal cords. It echoed along the tracks. He did it again and Taz joined him, like dogs howling at the moon. Taz leaped across the tracks and grabbed his brother by the shirt, hauling him to his feet. Luke's face was flushed. His eyes glowed like he was high on something.

Taz grabbed both sides of his brother's face and pressed their foreheads together. They stood in a headlock until Luke's legs stopped shaking.

I sat on the hill while they walked back to the skatepark, arms over each other's shoulders. "Ben, come on!" Luke turned and yelled for me; his grin like an open door.

Slowly, I got up and ambled towards them shaking my head in disbelief. The train could have flattened him, but Luke was oblivious. A euphoric glow and the sharp tang of sweat clung to them. I felt like I'd joined a party too late.

"That was insane!" Taz slapped his brother on the back and shook him a little.

Luke basked in the attention. He turned to me and waited for my praise. "Yeah, insane," I muttered without meeting his eyes.

The kids around the bowl shouted and clapped when they saw Luke. Taz pretended to be a sports announcer and gave a play-by-play of Luke Dumont versus The Train. I hung back, watching. What would have happened if he hadn't made it across the last time?

On the other side of the skatepark, Cory caught my eye and motioned for me. He'd just arrived with Kira Grayeyes. She sat beside him, her long legs bent so her chin rested on her knee. She gave me a faint smile, the corners of her eyes crinkling. I tried to stand taller, but compared to Cory, I looked, and felt, like a boy.

"The kid okay?" He asked with a chin-nod towards Luke. Five kids who had just arrived surrounded Luke as he re-enacted the race against the train in a clumsy slow-motion action sequence.

The wind lifted my shaggy blond hair out of my eyes and I nodded.

"Was it Taz's idea?" Kira asked. She pressed her lips together and tilted her head waiting for my response.

"Yeah."

Kira shook her head. "They're crazy."

Cory snorted.

"They are," Kira said and widened her eyes at Cory. "It's like they have a death wish or something. Especially Taz." She grabbed his shoulder. "And you're no better, so don't pretend you are."

Cory smirked at her and hopped off the rock, pulling her down too. She was almost as tall as he was and looked him in the eye with her hands on her hips, like a disapproving mom. "You love it," he said to Kira, wrapping an arm around her waist and kissing her.

"I should go," I said, as if they cared I was still there. I'd started walking around the bowl when Cory caught up to me. He went right down into the bowl ignoring the kids skating. No one said anything and altered their paths, wheels scraping against the concrete as they swerved to avoid him.

Luke's head was thrown back in laughter. "You owe me a movie, dude!" He grinned at Taz. "And I get to take your truck!" A whoop of delight flew from his lips.

One corner of Taz's lip curled and he cuffed Luke on the back of the head. "I'm coming with you, moron. You think I'd let you take my truck and hitch home?"

Luke rubbed his head and eyed his brother, the smile dying on his face. Hanging back a few feet, I saw Cory move between Luke and Taz.

"Did you see it, Cory? I beat the train, man!"

Cory raised an eyebrow, but didn't look impressed and let Luke's words hang there, unanswered. Did he agree with Kira, that the brothers had a death wish, or was he pissed that Luke's recklessness hadn't involved him?

He rolled his head around a few times cracking his neck. "So are we going to the movie or what?" A slow smile spread across his face. "We can go to that new parking garage after." He smiled.

"What parking garage?" Luke asked.

I knew which one they meant. "The one by the movie theatre," I said. Still under construction, it wouldn't be ready until the fall. It was just a skeleton of steel joists and posts. A chain link fence surrounded it to keep people out, but I didn't think that was a problem for Cory and Taz.

Cory glanced at me. "Is he cool?" he asked Luke.

Luke shrugged and nodded, "He saved my weed, remember?"

"I thought we could, you know," he put his fingers to his mouth as if he held an imaginary cigarette and inhaled.

I wanted to walk away. But my feet were rooted to the spot where I stood. Luke's grin spread wider and he laughed in anticipation. I swear, half the time he seemed stoned anyway.

Compared to these guys, my experiences with drinking and drugs were pretty limited. Tessa and I had stolen beer from her brother a couple of years ago. We'd giggled as we drank each can in long gulps behind some bushes at her house. It had tasted like warm piss, or what I thought warm piss would taste like. Another time, she found some pot in her oldest brother's room. It looked like dried oregano, but the smell gave it away. We'd used a piece of loose-leaf to roll it. After coughing and spitting out the chemical taste of ink and burnt paper and sitting around staring at a tree for a while, we decided skateboarding was enough of a high.

They headed back to the truck. Now was my chance to leave, find Tessa and say sorry.

Luke yelled for me, "Come on!" Getting in Taz's truck meant a summer job. And being one of the cool kids, part of a group, not the loner with a chick for a friend.

Tessa was already mad at me. What did it matter if I went to a movie? What was the worst that could happen?

The movie theater parking lot was packed. A guy in a sports car gave Taz the finger when he snaked a parking spot.

"Why wait?" Cory asked, pulling a joint from his pocket. "I've got another one for later."

His lighter flared as he held it under the joint and inhaled deeply, rolling his head against the seat and passed it to Taz. Luke grabbed it from his brother and put it to his lips quickly, taking only a short, shallow puff and gave it to me. I put the joint to my lips and pretended to take a hit, holding my breath and coughing as I exhaled. The truck quickly filled with smoke and Taz opened the window a crack. I'd have to throw my clothes in the wash as soon as I got home. If Mom smelled pot on my clothes, I'd be grounded for weeks.

Even though I'd only pretended to take a hit off the joint, sitting in the truck with its heavy haze swirling around my head made me feel lighter, like I was floating to the theatre, not walking. With a goofy grin plastered to my face, even the rude comments Taz shouted at girls seemed a little funny and my laughter echoed Cory and Luke's. I was with it enough to notice the way other kids turned to stare at us when we walked in. Girls checked us out over their shoulders, looking through their lashes at Cory's confident strut.

Unfurling a crumpled bill, I paid and stuffed the ticket and change into the pocket of my jeans. Ducking through the crowd, I found Luke, Taz and Cory joking around in the line by the theatre doors. Their yips and snarls echoed against the pinging of videogames and electronic rock music. The dopey haze was wearing off and I stood to the side, clutching my board and breathing in the thick, buttery smell of popcorn, wishing I had enough money to buy some.

I didn't see Jim until he was almost beside me. The too tight jeans on the woman he was with caught my eye first. I guess I'd been staring because the woman glared at me like she was going to pick a fight if I didn't look away. Jim turned around. He'd brushed his hair into a soft, furry nest that curved around his head.

He looked at me like he knew me, but couldn't remember how. The fact that he could make the time to take some chick on a date, but not to see me, was like a slap in the face.

I'm your son, I wanted to hiss at him, *the one who's not worth seeing*. "Hey," I said, trying to keep my face as blank as possible.

Jim burst into a nervous a chuckle and clamped a hand on my shoulder. "Ben! What are you doing here?"

"Watching a movie," I said and flinched at his touch. Could he smell the pot? I took a few steps away from him and his hand fell off my shoulder.

Clearing his throat, he said, "This is my son, Ben." The woman's face instantly changed and she beamed at me. Her teeth were white against her orangey-tan skin and I wondered if they'd glow in the dark movie theater. "Ben, this is Sheri."

I let my hair fall down over my eyes and gave her a chin nod. "Hey."

The guys had pushed their way up to the front of the line. Cory shoved Taz and he bumped into the girl behind him and some of her popcorn spilled. The two of them erupted into laughter. A security guard wandered over, standing in front of them with hairy arms crossed in front of his bulky chest. Even a few feet away, I could see the gleam in Cory's eyes.

"Those your friends?" My dad asked with a nod in their direction. Standing beside Sheri, he looked old and wrinkly. His eyes were almost hidden by folds of sagging skin and his nose glowed red.

"Yeah." At least he'd see that other people wanted to spend time with me.

Cory pushed Luke and he fell into a garbage can. It wobbled, and when Luke grabbed it for support, he tumbled to the ground. Cory started to laugh so hard he wiped tears from his eyes. A smile crept onto my face too. Taz held out a hand to help his brother up, but instead of taking it, Luke reached over and yanked on Taz's pants. They hung so low anyway, that it didn't take much for them to drop to his ankles. A few people laughed, but most backed away. The security guard reached for his radio.

Dad looked at me and smiled, like we shared some secret bond. I didn't smile back. Sheri looked like she wanted leave and pressed herself against the wall as two more security guards pushed past us and surrounded Taz, Luke and Cory.

Taz shouted, "Like hell! We're not going anywhere." He stood up and butted up against one of the guards.

The security guard put his hands on his hips and puffed out his chest. "You are causing a disturbance. We will refund your money, but you need to vacate the premises, or we will call the police." His deep, authoritative voice was ruined by his lisp.

"Oooooh! Premitheth! You're going to kick me off the 'premitheth'!" Taz held his stomach in a fit of laughter as he mocked the guard.

"Let's go." Each of the guards grabbed one of my friends under the arm and rotated him towards the emergency exit, which was directly behind me. Still laughing hysterically, none of them tried to resist.

"Hey, they were just having fun!" Dad called to the security guard. He rolled his eyes at me as if the injustice was too much for him.

"Ben!" Luke said as he was dragged past. "We're getting kicked out!" The joint had left his eyes watery and both lids hung lazily like he was about to fall asleep. The security guard hip-checked the door open and a blast of cool air hit me. The guard pushed Luke out the door, followed by Cory and Taz.

Dad's musky breath was at my ear. "You can watch the movie with us, if you want." Even with the minty breath fresheners, the tanginess of beer hung on his breath.

The Fall

I backed away from him. "He's my ride," I said and gestured at Taz. The guard held the door open, waiting for me to follow.

Dad nodded and moved back beside Sheri whose face had changed again. She looked at me like I was a dangerous animal. Ducking under the security guard's arm, and catching a dose of underarm odor, I joined Luke, Taz and Cory outside.

The door thudded and clicked behind us, sealing us out of the theatre. I thought of Dad and his girlfriend on the other side. I wondered if he'd think about me while he watched the movie. He'd acted like everything was fine between us. He could have at least apologized for not showing up the other day, but I guess he didn't want to look like a deadbeat in front of his girlfriend. I wished I'd told him off, right in front of his girlfriend. With the door shut between us, all the things I could have said hammered through my head.

"That was bullshit, man!" Cory spat at the door. "That fat dude was watching us since we walked in. He just wanted an excuse to kick us out! It was your board." He pointed at me. "They hate it when kids bring them in."

I didn't point out that Luke had knocked over a garbage can and they'd all acted like assholes.

"We should tag this place!" Luke said, "Later tonight, when everybody's gone. That would teach them not to mess with us!"

"Nah, I'd rather just catch that fat bastard on his way to his car after work and—" Cory smashed his fist into his palm and gave a throaty laugh.

Taz had lost interest in getting revenge and pointed to the construction site next to the theatre. "Come on, let's go smoke the other joint."

"Hey, I'm gonna grab a bus home." After getting kicked out of the theatre and seeing my dad, I wanted to be alone.

The three of them looked at me. Cory shrugged, "Suit yourself." He and Taz kept walking.

"Yeah, me too," Luke said. It caught me off-guard and I stared at him.

"Don't you want to hang out with your brother?"

"Nah, it's cool. I'll just crash at your place tonight."

It wasn't cool. Mom would freak out if Luke came in smelling like weed. Or worse if she got home from work and found him sleeping on the couch. I didn't want to deal with Mom being pissed at me. Tessa was enough. With a silent groan, I gave him a half smile. "Actually, I will hang out for a while. Kind of early to go home." Maybe once he started smoking some pot, he'd be too stoned to notice if I left.

Luke's face broke into a grin. "Yeah! Don't want to miss out on a few sweet tokes, right dude? Me neither."

Gripping my board tighter in frustration, I nodded.

We caught up to Taz and Cory at the chain link fence surrounding the construction site. A heavy padlock strung through two thick chains ensured that kids like us wouldn't be able to get in. Taz yanked the locks and dropped them with a rattle against the fence.

"Let's jump it. Give the skater a boost," Cory ordered. Taz crouched down so I could step on his back. What the hell? I didn't want to be the one to go over first, this wasn't even my idea.

"My board." How could I climb the fence holding it? Cory grabbed it and tossed it over the fence like it was a piece of garbage. It bounced and landed against a port-a-potty, but didn't break. He smirked at me. "Better go get it." My cheeks blazed, but I gritted my teeth and stepped on Taz's back, then stretched to touch the top. "Stand up a bit," Cory told Taz. "He can't reach." Taz's legs trembled under my weight.

The sharp points of the chain stabbed my palm as I heaved my body over the top and dropped to the other side, a cloud of dust puffed up around me when I landed. "Find something to open the gate with," Cory ordered. "Wire snips or a hacksaw or something." I ignored him and went to my board, spinning the wheels to make sure there was no damage.

"What's that?" He pointed to a pair of rusty, long handled bolt cutters lying beside a yellow construction helmet. "Try to cut the fence with them."

After a few snips, Cory peeled back a corner of the fence so Taz and Luke could crawl under and then went through himself. They stood, brushing dirt off their hands and knees and surveying the site.

In the dying daylight, the skeleton of a four-story parking garage loomed over us. Steel girders crisscrossed each other in a three-dimensional grid. The top level was covered by corrugated metal sheets, and a grid of rebar not yet covered with cement coiled around the exterior of the building. A maze of scaffolding covered the backside of the building. Traffic noises, honks and accelerating motors, filled the air, but the site was still, except for us.

Cory made a leap for the scaffolding and grabbed on to the lowest level, hauling himself up like a swimmer out of a pool. "Come on," he taunted, looking at Taz. "Let's go sit on the roof and smoke the joint."

I looked up to the top of the scaffolding. If construction workers climbed up and down, it could hold us. The other guys went first, following Cory who climbed higher, zigzagging through the metal beams and cross bars until he reached the top. I was still on solid ground. Setting my board on the ground beside me, I took a deep breath and jumped up onto the wooden plank. By the time I'd climbed up one level of scaffolding, Taz and Luke had made it to the top and bellowed the same whoop I'd heard at the train. They fist-bumped me when I reached them. It was hard work and we were all breathing heavy. Four stories was a long way up. Our feet echoed across sheets of corrugated metal as we clomped around. Sometimes a piece would shift or buckle, sending a vibration through the rest. "Hey, watch this!" Luke stood near the edge and undid his fly. A trickle of pee arced through the air and then separated as gravity pulled each droplet apart. He pulled up his zipper and turned to us with a dopey-eyed, wide-mouthed grin.

Taz curled his lip in mild disgust, as if someone had farted.

"Hey, over here!" Cory called from the other side of the roof. He sat on the edge, with his legs dangling over. It was a bad patchwork job and the metal sheets didn't entirely cover the top. Between the gaps I could peer down into the bowels of the structure. It was windier at the top than it had been on the ground and my hair floated into my face. I didn't want to brush it out of my eyes, nervous that I'd lose my balance and slide off the edge.

Gingerly, I walked towards Cory keeping my eyes glued to the peaks and valleys of the metal. He had dug some pennies out of his pocket and tossed them at a metal hydro pole. They hit with a ping, the noise echoing in the stillness four stories up.

Eight crows sat on a wire, fixated on the movie theatre parking lot. Their shiny black feathers glistened purple-blue in the streetlights, like motor oil in a puddle.

A whole section of the metal sheeting was missing and the only way to cross was to balance across a steel girder. Trust Cory to force us to follow him across a chasm. I hung back, checking out the view of the city from four stories up. A few tall buildings rose up from downtown and the river, swollen from the spring thaw, twisted, muddied and churning, like a snake through the city. Cars raced over the bridge connecting both sides of the city. From up there, I could even see where the sprawl ended and gave way to wide open fields.

Taz gave a groan of impatience and moved past me, stepping across the girder like it was a balance beam two feet off the ground, not four stories in the air. I counted his steps. He'd crossed in eight.

Luke was next. He peered over the edge. "Come on," Taz jeered from the other side. "Don't be a pussy."

Luke turned to look at me. His eyes were wide with fear and he'd gone pale. I wanted to reach out to him and make him follow me to the ground. I opened my mouth to say something, but he'd already turned back to his brother.

He took a tentative step on the beam. His shoes were red. Red skater shoes with thick, flat soles and a wide, gaping space for the laces. I held my breath for him as he put his other foot on the beam. Taz stood on the other side watching. His face tense. Luke's breath came in short, jagged spurts.

"This isn't so hard," he said, his voice full of confidence. He looked up at Taz, who gave him a lopsided grin back. I saw his shoulders relax when he'd made it more than halfway across.

Cory, his back to us must have grown bored of flicking coins at the pole, because he'd turned his attention to the birds. I kept my eyes trained on Luke. Only a couple more steps. I felt myself exhale. He was going to make it.

The crows suddenly took flight, in a burst of squawking and flapping, they rose off the wire and above our heads. Luke threw his head back, as if startled by the commotion, and lost his balance. Flinging his arms out to steady himself, they windmilled in the air and his body tilted.

My chest collapsed as all the air got sucked out of my lungs.

The white rubber on the bottom of Luke's sneakers shone as his body fell backwards, floating in the sky like a slow motion kung fu movie.

I stood helplessly an arm's length away.

The fall seemed instant. One second he was tipping over and in the next he was a crumpled heap at the bottom of the parking garage.

I scrambled down the scaffolding and swung between the never-ending bars to reach the ground. "Oh-God-oh-God-oh-God!" my breath pounded in my ears. Cory and Taz swore as they crossed back over the beam, their feet heavy and frantic on the sheets of metal.

Dropping onto the gravel at the bottom, I raced to Luke. Cory and Taz skidded to a stop beside me, kicking up a cloud of dust. In the shadowy light, their faces glowed white with shock. Luke was still. A trickle of blood dribbled out of his mouth and ran down his chin, but his eyes were open. They focused on Taz. "Ohhhhhh," he groaned, but it wasn't a normal groan. It was like his body was forcing the air out of his lungs. "Shit," he whispered. His head lolled to one side and went still.

A noise I'd never heard before, a deep, rasping growl, like a motor grinding, broke through the silence. I didn't know it was me until I fell to the ground at Luke's feet. They were splayed at weird angles and one red shoe lay a few meters away. Taz and Cory stared at me and Cory burst out laughing. Taz stood up and backed away from his brother.

"Oh, shit!" Cory broke into hysterical giggles. His eyes never left Luke's face until he threw up.

Taz had buried his face in his hands and was pacing between two poles. Everything moved around me in a haze. I was conscious of what they were doing, but it was like I was watching them on TV. We were all trapped in invisible boxes near each other, but too far away to connect.

"Get up. You're freaking me out," Cory ordered me. He wiped saliva and vomit off his chin and spit into the corner. Shaking his head like an animal drying off, he looked at Taz.

"Call an ambulance," I mumbled, standing up.

They ignored me.

"Call an ambulance!" I shouted.

Taz kept pacing, his feet wearing a path between the two poles.

Cory took his phone out of his pocket. His hands shook and he couldn't flip it open. Tossing it to the ground, he walked in a circle and came back beside me. We both stood staring down at Luke. A wave of warmth rolled up from my stomach and I turned around to retch into a pile of gravel. Nothing came up, but I crouched near the ground shivering.

Cory picked up his phone. His voice cracked and stuck in his throat. "My friend … he fell. I think he's," his voice caught and I heard him retch behind me. With a shaking breath, I turned around and took the phone from him.

"Hello? Hello? Are you there?" the 911 operator asked.

"Uh, yeah. He fell. We need an ambulance." My voice didn't sound real. It was like someone else's a million miles away. I didn't let myself look anywhere near Luke. The only way I would be able to finish the call was if I pretended to be somewhere else. I stared at the streetlights peering over the parking lot like aliens, the bulbous heads too big for the skinny bodies.

"Where are you?" her voice sounded more alert. I could hear the clicking of computer keys in the background.

"We're at the new parking garage by the movie theatre off Route 30."

"Okay, I'm sending help. Is he conscious?"

"No."

She kept me on the line with more questions, but I let the phone drop when the fire truck arrived, its horn blaring and lights flashing. The red strobe exploded against the metal beams disappearing and appearing. It was hypnotizing.

I stood back. The firemen swarmed like ants, focused, each with a job to do. They pushed us out of the way to get to Luke.

By the time the cops arrived, the three of us stood against the chain link fence like convicts. A woman cop and her partner got out of the car. "I'm Constable MacIsaac. You boys want to tell me what happened here?" I swallowed and hoped she didn't drive us home. My mom always said if I was ever driven home in a cop car, I might as well keep driving. I hoped she was joking, but you never know.

"Boys?" she raised an eyebrow and cocked her head.

I cleared my throat. Cory shot me a warning glance. Constable MacIsaac shifted her stance so Cory wasn't in my line of vision. "We were just goofing off. We climbed up to the top, but then Luke slipped…."

She kept staring at me as if there was more. But that was it. Just the fall.

"Is that how you remember it?" she turned to Cory. He nodded.

Taz bellowed a long, low moan like an animal caught in a trap. "It was me. It was my fault!" The cop's head snapped towards him, her eyes bright and attentive. "He followed me. He always follows me!" Taz shouted it like an accusation. Strings of spittle sprayed from his mouth. "Oh, God!" His legs buckled.

Constable MacIsaac motioned for her partner, a younger cop, to check on Taz. "We're going to have to ask you boys more questions. Have you called your parents yet?" I shook my head.

The Fall

Luke, loaded onto a gurney, was wheeled past us. His head rolled side to side, bumping over the uneven ground. Taz doubled over and lurched after him. "Where are you taking him?" he shouted. The paramedics ignored him, walking past as if he was a ghost. The female cop barred him from getting closer, stopping him with a raised arm.

"To the hospital."

Taz stumbled. "I gotta stay with him!" He looked at her, shaking and pleading. "He's my brother, I gotta stay with him!"

Empathy flashed across her face. She turned to the open ambulance door. Luke's gurney was being lifted up, the wheels tucking under in one smooth motion. The man at the door glanced over and gave a nod of his head. "Go," she said to Taz. "We'll meet you there."

Taz flung himself into the ambulance and then froze, staring down at his brother, lifeless on the cot. The ambulance doors shut with finality and the siren began to wail. I glimpsed Cory out of the corner of my eye. He clenched his jaw, the lines knife sharp and his face ghoulish in the pulsating red light of the ambulance. His expression didn't change as they drove away.

She looked at Cory and I. "You two can come with us. Your parents can pick you up at the hospital."

My mouth had gone dry. "Which hospital?" I croaked, licking my lips. "My mom works at St. Vic's."

"That's where we're going. She working tonight?"

I nodded.

"Okay. We'll let her know when you get there." Part of me wanted to see my mom, but all of me wanted to run away and pretend this night had never happened.

St. Vic's Hospital was a few minutes away, but the driving there felt like forever. My stomach twisted in knots while Cory sat still as stone beside me. Luke must have already been rushed inside, because when we got to the hospital, the ambulance was gone.

The cops ushered us into a room with orange vinyl chairs and blotchy linoleum tiles. Taz was already there, but didn't look up when we walked in. Where was Luke? In a room somewhere? Alone?

The room smelled like cleaning solution and a package of band-aids; the same smell that lingers on Mom's uniform after work. A water tank in the corner gurgled every few minutes as a bubble burped through the tank. Nobody said anything. We sat staring at our shoes waiting for the next bubble of water to float to the top and explode.

Mom arrived first. Wide-eyed and flushed, her ID badge bobbed against the pocket of her uniform as she raced into the waiting area. "Oh, Ben!" She grabbed the back of my neck and pulled me against her. Hot tears burned behind my eyes, but I didn't let them spill out. Not in front of Taz.

Constable MacIsaac told me I could go. I stood up, my legs weak and shaking with relief. Mom laid an arm across my shoulders and hugged me against her. I looked at Cory and Taz slumped in the chairs, waiting for their parents. What if Taz's mom and dad didn't want to see him? How do you go from saying goodbye to one son, to taking the other one home?

I opened my mouth to say something, but no sound came. They didn't look up as I walked out of the room.

TAZ

The room stayed silent after Ben left. Taz's saliva tasted thick and acidic. He wondered if he'd he thrown up. Smudges of dirt and blood covered his hands, but he couldn't remember if it was his own, or his brother's.

"Taz?" The female cop said when his dad entered the room. "You can go." As she moved aside, Taz glanced at his father's face, pale and haggard, like a beat up old hound dog, and then stared at the ground. He didn't see his dad raise his hand, but felt the back of it catch him across the cheek. A red welt flared up.

"Sir!" The cop spoke sharply, and escorted them to the hall where his mom was waiting. Slumped in a chair, she erupted into wails when she saw Taz. Her face was swollen, and unrecognizable. She fell against Taz in a slobbering mess, her tears, spit and snot leaving a shiny trail on his shirt. His dad walked to the exit. When the doors magically opened for him, he turned around and barked, "Come on!" Taz maneuvered his mom down the hall, stumbling under her dead weight.

His dad stood by their minivan. "Gimme your keys." His voice was hoarse.

Taz looked at him puzzled. His truck was still at the movie theatre.

"Gimme your goddamned keys!" Mr. Dumont said again.

Reaching into his pocket, Taz passed them to his father. With a sneer, his father tossed the keys across the street. No one heard them land over the wail of a siren and the flow of traffic.

"What the hell? Why'd you do that?" Taz turned on his father, eyes wide with shock. He'd never find them in the dark.

"Your brother never had a truck, and now neither do you."

Mr. Dumont opened his door and heaved his bulk inside.

"I have a spare set, asshole," Taz muttered under his breath. He knew his dad would be able to find them if he wanted, but didn't care. What did his truck matter now, anyway? He'd have given it away in a heartbeat to have Luke back again.

Thursday

CORY

Cory lay in bed. His arm flung across his eyes.

We should have dug a pit and buried him. Calling the cops after Luke fell had been a mistake. He'd hated waiting in the room at the hospital for his mom. When she'd finally shown up, she wouldn't look at him.

And the silence in the car on the way home had been deafening.

Maybe it's a good thing he died. Better than being paralyzed or a vegetable attached to machines for the rest of his life. Maybe Luke was supposed to die young. When your time is up, it's up. At least, that's what someone had said to him when his dad died.

"Cory?" His sister, Michelle, opened his bedroom door without knocking. The lock had been removed last year by his mom. He usually remembered to move a heavy piece of furniture in front of the door so she couldn't barge in. "Is it true? About Luke?" Her brown eyes were wide with curiosity. She looked like a female version of Cory. They had the same cheekbones and dark slash of eyebrows.

Cory jammed his head under the pillow. Michelle called his name again, louder and whinier.

"How'd you find out?" He tossed the pillow aside, his face ashen and his voice empty.

She backed away, peering at him. "It's all over Facebook. Simon Wolf's dad is a cop and he told Simon about Luke. I guess Simon posted it as soon as he found out."

Cory's eyes gave her the answer.

"What happened?" she gasped.

"What the hell do you care, you didn't even know him." She made a move to sit on the side of his bed, but he kicked his feet out.

"Oh my God, were you there?"

Like a kick to his gut, Luke's inert body flashed in front of his eyes. "I said, eff off!" She stood in the middle of his room, too shocked to move. Cory closed his eyes and turned his back to her. For a few moments, the only sound in the room was their breathing. When Michelle finally left, Cory looked at the time. Luke had only fallen twelve hours ago and already it was up on Facebook.

Throwing off the blanket, Cory planted his feet on the floor and waited for the room to stop spinning. The mirror told an ugly story. He looked like he hadn't slept in a month, his bloodshot eyes had deep bluish smudges under them. Turning on the computer, he logged on to Facebook.

Taz hadn't posted anything. Neither had Ben. Random kids who barely knew Luke had made RIP signs and wrote things like "I love you, Luke." Cory snorted at their insincerity. He knew people would start asking questions soon. Why had they been up there? Whose idea was it? Why had Luke fallen? People would blame him or Taz. They were the wild ones. They had a reputation.

Cory grit his teeth, trying to remember why he hadn't seen Luke fall.

He'd crossed the beam first and, too impatient to wait for the others, had gone to sit on the edge of the roof. He remembered spotting the birds, their round skulls a tempting target, and fishing coins from his pocket. The first two had missed, but the third, it had made a concussive crack as it hit the crow's head, sending the flock into a riot of flapping. He'd turned to catch the expression on the other's faces, just as Luke tipped.

His pulse quickened. Had it been the birds? The birds he'd hit? The sound of them squawking and swooping echoed in his head. He clenched his jaw against the bile that rose in his throat. Had Taz or Ben realized it was his fault? He didn't think so, but his heart pounded. He had to fix it, push the blame to someone else. Cracking his knuckles, he started typing his version of Luke's fall.

BEN

We got home a little after midnight and I lay in bed, staring at the ceiling for hours.

He'd been a few feet away from me. I could have reached out to grab his hand, pulled him to safety. Instead, I'd just stood there, watching as he fell. He'd wanted to leave with me before we even got to the parking garage. What if we'd left then and taken a bus back to my house? He'd be snoring on the couch, not lying on a metal table covered by a sheet. Thoughts thudded through my head, landing with a bang. They grew heavier and heavier until I thought I'd suffocate under their weight.

Mom was in the kitchen. I could smell salty bacon frying and my stomach started to rumble. Wobbling down the hallway, I grabbed onto a kitchen chair and collapsed. "Thought you'd want to eat eventually," Mom said as she scrambled eggs.

She put the plate on the table and pulled out a chair to sit beside me, a mug of coffee in her hands. The bacon was overcooked, as usual, and shattered when I took a bite. It fell like confetti on my eggs. She slurped her coffee while I chewed. The eggs were tasteless no matter how much salt I added. Mopping up the grease with a piece of toast, I sat back in my chair.

"How are you feeling?" she asked.

I shrugged. "Like it didn't happen. Like I dreamed it."

"Did you see him fall?"

Nodding, I stared at the swirls of grease on my plate, tracking the pattern I'd made with my toast. It looked like a fingerprint. "He was walking across a steel beam and lost his balance. It happened so fast." The food settled uncomfortably in my stomach and I wondered if I was going to throw up. "How come I'm not crying?"

Mom reached a hand across the table and laid it on my arm. "You're still in shock." She leaned toward me. "Why were you up there?"

"It was Cory's idea." I couldn't look at Mom, so I stared at my hands. "I didn't want to go up there, but they were my ride home." That wasn't true. I could have left before we climbed. Luke would have come with me. He'd still be alive. Thinking about it made my chest hurt, like someone was stepping on it and I couldn't get enough air.

She took my plate. The cutlery clattered as she dumped it in the sink. "I took today and tomorrow off."

I looked at her in surprise. "You don't have to babysit me."

"I know." She wiped her hands on the dishtowel and stared at me for a minute. "It's been a while since I saw you skate. I thought we could go downtown to that new skatepark that opened in the warehouse."

I shook my head. "No, thanks." How could I skate when I'd seen a guy drop to his death? What kind of an asshole goes out to have fun after that?

"Maybe later?" she asked.

I shrugged, my body felt sluggish and heavy, like each limb was caked in cement. "I'm going back to bed."

"Ben?"

I stopped in the kitchen doorway and turned to her. Mom's eyes were droopy and sad. She was a nurse. She'd seen people die before. But never a friend. Never someone who wasn't supposed to.

"You're allowed to do normal things, like skate. It might help."

I couldn't imagine ever feeling normal again. Were Cory and Taz doing normal things? Sleeping? Eating? Talking? As if they hadn't seen Luke die in front of them? Would feeling the mind numbing rhythm of concrete under my board dull the jagged flashes of memory?

Maybe Mom was right, Benjiland would be an escape. At least for a little while. But right now, all I wanted was sleep.

This time I slept. Hard. I woke up and didn't know where I was. It took me a minute to remember why I was waking up at three in the afternoon.

I changed out of my sweats and t-shirt into jeans and a clean-ish hoodie. My board rested against the wall behind my door. I ran a hand over the deck's nose. The plywood was rough with splinters and would have to be replaced soon. I inspected the trucks. The metal was gouged and worn. New ones were expensive and Mom wanted me to get a job to help with bills, not for new gear. I gave the wheel a spin and stared at it, hypnotized.

I'd watched Luke die, but I was worrying about new trucks for my skateboard. How eff'd up was that? Mom was right, going to the skatepark would clear my head, help me straighten out. Maybe if I was in Benjiland, I'd stop seeing the look of shock on Luke's face as he tipped over and then the horror when he realized he was falling.

As I stared out the car window, my stomach twisted in knots. The sky hung gray and grimy, like dirty water. Mom drummed her fingers on the steering wheel to a folksy rock song. "Tessa's mad at me."

Mom stopped drumming and turned down the radio. "Why?"

Propping my elbow against the window, I rested my forehead in my palm. "I bailed on her last night and went out with those guys instead. Now she hates me."

"She doesn't hate you," Mom said shaking her head. "She's your best friend. Her feelings were hurt."

"She's going to rub it in so hard because she warned me about those guys."

Mom threw a quick look at me. "Maybe you should text her."

I shrugged.

"Don't play games, Ben." There was a warning tone in her voice.

"I saw Dad at the movies."

Mom raised her eyebrows. "Did you talk to him?"

"Yeah. But, it was weird."

She smirked. "Try being married to him." With a glance at me, her tone changed. "What did he say?"

I snorted and put my feet up on the dash, resting my head against the back of the seat. "I don't remember." Wanting Dad's attention felt trivial compared to Luke's last, gurgly breath. In fact, nothing mattered anymore. Dad, Tessa, school, a job. I was numb to everything.

The skatepark was in an old warehouse. Murals by graffiti artists covered the red brick exterior and the metal door had been tagged with 'SK*t'. I heaved it open and stepped inside.

"I'll be over there," Mom said pointing to the observation area. I nodded, but part of me didn't want her to leave my side. With weak legs, I walked to a bench and put on my helmet and pads. The sooner I found my way to Benjiland, the better. A two story half pipe at one end. Rails. Steps. A platform. Two bowls that connected. I felt myself come alive as my mind swam with ideas of my board flying over the course. Inhaling the smell of fresh concrete, I dropped my board in.

Tessa would love this. There weren't any other girls skating. I wanted to text her to join me, but couldn't. How could I look her in the face when she'd warned me about hanging out with those guys?

It had only been a day since I'd skated, but my legs felt stiff. I took a few runs around the bowl. It was like swimming with a current, if you relax and let the current guide you instead of fighting against it you'll go further. I let the bowl tell me where to push off and when to lean in and started to gain speed. Coming up to the half-pipe, I sailed off and reached between my legs to grab the heel of the board and pulled it towards my back. A meter in the air, nothing mattered but me and my board.

I skated until my legs were weak.

"Hey," A guy with a shaved head crouched beside me as I unsnapped my helmet and knee pads. He wore a black t-shirt with the Rox skate store label on it. "What's your name?"

I hesitated, trying to place him. He looked familiar. "Ben."

"How long you been skating?" He eyed my board.

"About eight years."

"Oh yeah? You looked good out there. I'm Ev. My buddy and I own Rox."

I stopped fiddling with my chinstrap and gave him my full attention.

"Does Mitch know you?"

"Yeah, I'm in the store a lot. You hang out more in the back, right?"

With a grin he said, "I'm more the brains of the operation, but don't tell Mitch. I do marketing, sponsoring, that kind of thing. No promises, but we're looking for a young skater to sponsor. And you have talent." He reached into his back pocket and gave me a business card. "Call me tomorrow. I want Mitch to see you skate."

"Okay, yeah," I said as coolly as possible. Putting his card in my pocket, I hoped he didn't notice my hand shaking. He walked away and waved at some older guys getting ready to ride the half-pipe. I laughed to myself, hardly believing what had just happened.

"Hey, Mom."

She folded down the page of her book with a guilty look. "I was watching, I promise. I just started reading when you stopped."

"Did you see that guy talking to me?" I grinned, my cheeks glowing.

"No, who?"

"The guy in charge of sponsorships for Rox. Mom, this is huge! He wants the other owner to see me skate. They might sponsor me."

"They want to pay you to skate? Like a professional athlete?"

I couldn't wipe the smile off my face. "Not in money, but in gear. Like I'd wear their clothes and they'd help me out with my board and wheels and stuff and enter me in contests." A new wave of excitement swept over me at the thought of it. I wanted to run circles around the skatepark shouting at the top of my lungs 'Rox wants to sponsor me!' "Mom! This is huge!" I said again. She laughed.

"Okay, I get it, I get it! This is huge," she mimicked me. "You can tell me all about on the way home."

The skatepark had gotten busier while I'd been skating. Kids loitered at the entrance and most looked like they wanted a place to hang out more than skate. We walked past some who went to Tucker High. I did a double take. The girls were huddled together wiping away tears and some older guys stood together, muttering and shaking their heads. Had they already heard about Luke?

Excitement over Ev's offer disappeared, a heavy, guilt settled on me.

So easily, I'd forgotten Luke.

In a flash, I was back there again, swaying on the top of a four-story parking garage with a sick feeling in the pit of my stomach. The thud of Luke's body hitting the ground drowned out the slap of skateboards on concrete.

A few more kids walked up and joined the group. One girl held up a photo of Luke to her friend, who took it and held it to her heart.

I didn't realize I was staring until Mom yanked on my arm and pulled me through the door.

I rolled down the window in the car. The cool night air pulled me out of the fog. Images of Luke falling, his red shoe, his leg twisted, blood trickling out of his mouth, his last, garbled words and the vacant look in his eyes all flashed in front of me.

Horrible, wrenching cries exploded from my chest and out of my mouth. I couldn't catch my breath as my chest heaved. Squeezing my eyes shut, I pressed my knuckles to my forehead hard. So hard, it hurt more than everything else. Everything on the inside.

"Are you okay?" Mom squeezed my shoulder when we got to a red light.

I couldn't answer because I didn't know.

Friday

BEN

I fell into a deep, dark sleep that lasted until morning. When I woke up I felt like I didn't belong in my room, like I was a guest and the stuff in it didn't belong to me. I wasn't the same kid who had taped pictures of dudes flying through the air on their skateboards.

Mom was awake and rattling around in the kitchen. She watched me as I poured some juice.

"Since I have the day off, I thought we could go shopping. You need new jeans, I saw the holes in your favourite pair when I washed them." She gave me a hopeful smile.

Lifting the glass to my mouth, I put it down without taking a sip and steadied myself on the counter. "Shopping?"

The smile faded and she nodded slowly.

I shook my head. "There might be kids there, like at SK*t." She made a move towards me, but I sidestepped her. "I can't handle seeing them." Squeezing the glass so hard I thought it would crack and explode in my hand, I tried to push the emotions down into a dark hole where I could bury them.

"Okay," she said quietly.

The lump lodged in my throat ached when I tried to swallow it. "I'm going back to bed." My room felt like a cocoon. Closing the door sealed me into its protective shell.

I checked my phone. Still nothing from Tessa. Part of me was relieved, it meant not having to explain Luke's fall or why I had been there. But I wanted to talk to her, or at least know that she wanted to talk to me.

There was a knock on my bedroom door. Mom walked in with a cinnamon roll sealed in plastic wrap. "I forgot to tell you that Mama Pal brought over some food. She thinks calories will cure everything."

Mom sat on the edge of my bed. "And, your teacher, Ms. Jimenez, called to see how you were doing. She said a lot of kids are in shock and they set up a grief centre in the library. I could take you, if you wanted to go and talk to someone."

I stared at her blankly. School? The last place I wanted to go was school.

"Or I could call your doctor. To talk. If you wanted?"

Dr. Yip? I hadn't seen him in three years. I wasn't going to start spilling my guts to some guy who didn't even know me.

She waited a few minutes, but when I didn't reply, she got up and set the plate on my dresser. "This room is a disaster," she said with a sigh and picked up a pair of jeans and shook them out. She bent down to pick up the coins and bits of paper that fell out of the pockets and passed them to me. I felt the bumpy, perforated edges of a movie ticket in my palm. As if I needed another reminder. A wave of emptiness washed over me, and my face crumpled in a rush of hot tears.

TAZ

The glass bottle in Taz's backpack thunked against his spine. He could hear the vodka swishing from side to side as he walked up Garbage Hill. Headlights from a few cars lit the slope, but weren't visible yet. He could hear bursts of laughter over the music pounding from car stereos. Taz walked blindly, squinting against the headlights shining in his face. When he got to the top of the hill, he took out his bottle, twisted off the cap and threw down his backpack.

"Tazzie!" One of the guys yelled. They were mostly older guys, done school and working in dead-end jobs. Hanging out on Garbage Hill every weekend night was their idea of a good time. Taz ignored the greeting and waited for the first swill of alcohol to burn down his throat. After the warmth sank in, the forgetting could start.

He'd walked here the night after Luke had fallen. The guys had greeted him with cheers, as if he were a returning war hero. They didn't know about Luke yet and thought the old Taz had shown up, the one with a loud laugh who liked to hurl insults and pick fights. The kind of guy you want at a night of drinking. Instead, they got a guy who sat by himself staring into the black at the bottom of the hill wondering what Luke felt when he fell. *Had his bones snapped when he hit the ground? Had his organs exploded? Had it hurt?*

"It's cold, man," a guy with ponytail said to him. He looked familiar, but it was dark out and his brain was getting cloudy. "I'm going to sit in the car." Not many people were left; only a few cars dotted the hill. Taz followed him, stumbled into the backseat and passed out.

When he woke up hours later, the air inside the car was hot, muggy and it stunk. He retched, it smelled so bad. His cheek made a squelching sound when he unstuck it from the vinyl upholstery. A wet splotch of drool was left behind. Grabbing for the door, Taz stuck his head out and threw up.

Thoughts and pictures were jumbled in Taz's head. Images floated by and he couldn't remember what day it was or how long it had been since his brother fell. A flash of memory came back to him: the social worker who'd come to his house that afternoon. She'd walked in the house and peered around corners like someone was going to jump out and bite her. She'd asked his parents to leave the room so she could talk to him. "Our house is the size of a trailer," he'd muttered. "They'll hear you no matter where they go."

She'd ignored his rudeness and soldiered on, taking out a file and pen. "How are you feeling, since your brother's death?"

Taz wasn't listening. He noticed she'd taken off her shoes at the door and even from his spot on the couch could see her toenails poking through her nylons. They looked yellow and pointy, like dog's teeth.

She'd asked again.

"Fine." *I'm not telling you a thing, lady.*

"Any trouble sleeping?"

"No." *I'm afraid to close my eyes because as soon as I do, I hear the birds squawking. They rose up like a storm cloud, swirling in the sky.*

"Is there anything you want to talk about, Taz?"

"Nope." *I hear his laugh and forget he's gone. I start to ask him what's so funny.*

"I want to tell you that after the shock of what happened wears off, you might be angry, sad or depressed. All those emotions are to be expected."

"Yep." *They flood my body. I grab my sides so hard to hold myself together there are bruises on my ribs.*

With another chug of whatever lay in the bottle beside him, Taz fell back onto the seat and slipped into black, blissful sleep.

The morning sun was bright when he woke up. The pain was still there. And Luke wasn't.

CORY

The day bled into night and back into morning. Michelle walked in his room with a set of keys dangling in her hand. "Mom says you can use the corvette if you drive me to dance class."

Cory took a deep breath. The corvette had been his dad's car. She held out the keys to him, spinning the key ring on her finger. She had no sense of how important that car was.

"Mom said she'd drive me, but she went to yoga with Elmer."

Cory rolled his eyes at the mention of Elmer, his mom's new boyfriend. He was rich, had a pot belly and drove a new car with chunky rims, the kind old men think look expensive.

Michelle stepped closer. "Please, Cory. My recital is in two weeks."

He groaned and rolled over.

"Let me change," he said and snatched the keys from her. He hadn't driven the corvette since last fall, when he'd taken the keys without asking. His mom had raged at him for stealing the car. He'd glowered at her, his eyes like darts. *Ask me why I took it*, he silently screamed. *I only remember his face when I'm driving his car. I can feel him beside me and I talk to him.* She'd hidden the keys, probably thrilled at finding one more way to punish him. Cory didn't know what was worse—that he'd seen his dad die in front of him, or that he'd walked away. Surviving the accident *was* the punishment, he had to face his widowed mom and fatherless sister every day of his life.

His mom had never said it, but he could tell when she looked at him, at the scar emblazoned on his forehead, that she'd never forgive him for being an arm's length away and letting his dad die.

The keys jingled in Cory's hand as he and Michelle walked to the garage. Cory slid into the driver's seat and brushed a finger along the dash. It needed to be polished. Michelle hopped in the other side and clicked her seat belt in place.

Turning the key in the ignition, the car purred to life with a deep hum that resonated against the cement garage walls. Cory turned the radio up as he reversed onto the street and a classic rock tune blasted through the speakers.

"I still can't believe what happened to Luke," she said, shaking her head at Cory. "It's just so weird to know that you were like, there, when someone died." Too late, she must have realized the cruelty of her words. Her hand flew to her mouth.

Again. The unspoken word hung between them, louder than the music booming from the radio. *How does she do that? Forget about it?* Cory had tried smoking pot, drinking, popping pills, but nothing worked. It wasn't the memory of the accident that left him hollow. It was looking at him mom's face when she remembered the accident. Or listening to Michelle talk as if his dad had never been there.

They'd been driving, not in the corvette, but in the car his dad took to work, and talking about music. "Let me play you a song," his dad had said and glanced down at the CD player for a second. In the same second, a car ran a red at the intersection; a silver bullet barreled into them.

The impact had spun them across two lanes of traffic and into a light post. Cory's head had banged against the window, but his seatbelt had held him in place. His dad, slumped over the steering wheel, had thick blood oozing down his face. A gurgling noise had come from his throat.

The paramedics tried to tell him later that his dad had died instantly. But Cory knew they were wrong. He'd seen his eyelids move. It had taken some minutes for the life to leak out of him and Cory had been right there, frozen in time while it happened.

"Cory!" Michelle shouted, tearing him away from his thoughts. He slammed his foot on the brake and they jolted forward. The car skidded to a stop at the red light. Michelle bit her lip, but didn't say anything.

Cory swore and pounded the steering wheel.

Michelle waited until the light turned green before she spoke again. "Did Mom tell you she and Elmer are driving to Calgary together this summer? He wants her to meet his kids." Cory knew this was the kind of thing his mom would spring on him at the last minute. "She wants me to ask a friend if I can stay with them while she's gone."

"Why don't you just stay at the house with me?"

"I already asked. She said she wants you to find somewhere else to stay too."

He snorted. "Good luck with that. I'm not getting kicked out of my own house because she wants a holiday. She cares more about the house than she does about us anyway." The house was a warren of rooms with fireplaces, and wood paneling. The biggest and oldest in the neighborhood, his parents had spent years renovating it; sanding down and staining every piece of trim, painting each room, rewiring the lights and polishing every brass door knob. There was as much of his dad in the house as there was in the coffin. After the accident, Cory wanted her to sell it, to move to a new neighborhood where no one knew him, where they could live in a bland cookie-cutter house void of memories. She'd refused. His dad's absence filled more space in the house than the three of them put together and he'd grown to hate it.

"No, she doesn't," Michelle argued.

"She only keeps it because I want her to sell it." Michelle stuck out her chin. "We were born there! A move would have been too stressful."

Cory looked at Michelle, "For who?"

"Do you like Elmer?" Michelle asked.

It seemed sacrilegious to talk about him in their dad's car.

"I think he's cheesy! Like his license plate, DRBONZ." She groaned.

Cory nodded. He'd spit a thick wad of saliva on Elmer's car the first time it had parked in the driveway.

"Do you think all chiropractors wear that much cologne? I can smell him before he rings the doorbell. Oh, that's the other thing. Mom gave him a key to the house. For emergencies, she said! Like one of us might sleep funny and need an emergency adjustment?"

Cory tuned her out and tapped his thumb to a Zeppelin song. His dad loved Led Zeppelin. Whenever one of their songs came on the radio, Cory hoped it was a sign his dad was watching over him.

If you're there, Dad. Fuck you for dying.

BEN

The TV droned in the family room. Its noise helped to block out my thoughts as I lay slumped on the couch, my feet on the coffee table. Mom sat across from me reading a book, glancing at me every few minutes. The phone rang, but I didn't make a move to get it. It had taken all my energy to drag myself from my room to the couch. Mom put down her book and went to pick up the phone. "Hello?" Her mouth set in a thin line. "Hang on." Her voice was tight when she passed the phone to me.

It was either Dad or a telemarketer. They both elicited the same response from Mom. I turned away from the phone and mouthed "No." Mom's eyes popped and she pushed the phone at me. "Tell him you don't feel well," she whispered. "He really wants to talk to you."

"Hello." My voice was flat, empty.

"Hey, Benny. Funny running into you the other night at the movies, eh? I just got off shift and heard something on the radio about a kid from Tucker High dying at a construction site. Hope he wasn't a friend of yours." The casualness of his tone knocked the wind of me.

"I was there."

There was a long pause.

"Oh, shit," he muttered. "I'm sorry … I didn't think … I just called because, well, I thought maybe I could see you sometime soon. You looked so big at the movies, I almost didn't recognize you."

That's what happens when you don't see me for months, I wanted to shout into the phone.

"Guess you're going through some things, eh?"

There was another long pause. "Yeah." My voice cracked and I didn't trust myself to say anymore.

"Yeah, okay. I get it. I just thought, well, I don't know what I thought," he laughed. At himself? At trying to have a relationship with me? Was he laughing at me? "You know where I am."

He hung up before I could say goodbye.

My phone buzzed with a text from Tessa after dinner. "Where the f r u?" read the first one, followed by "I'm comin ovr."

She stood on the front step glaring at me. Her pale skin glowed ghostly white under the porch light. "Can I come in, or what?"

"Hey. Nice to see you too," I said and moved aside. My eyes felt puffy and red from crying, but she didn't say anything.

Tessa brushed past me and went straight to my room, yelling "Hey, Mrs. O," over her shoulder.

"I'm still pissed at you," she said and tossed some clothes onto the floor so she could sit cross-legged on the desk chair.

"Tessa," I held up my hand to stop her talking. "If that's what you came over here to tell me, save it. I already feel like shit."

She shook her head. "No, I came to tell you I was an asshole." It was the closest to a sorry I was going to get from Tessa.

I blew out a breath and ran a hand through my hair, letting it flop down over my eyes. "I wish I hadn't gone anywhere with those guys."

She snorted in agreement. "Did Luke really fall because you scared him?"

"What?" I jerked my head up, thinking I hadn't heard her right.

"At school, everyone's talking about what Cory wrote on Facebook, something like 'never trust a skater'. He said you got them into the construction site and that Luke slipped because you scared him."

"That's not what happened," I shook my head, "Some birds flew up and he lost his balance." I stared at her in disbelief. "It was Cory's idea to climb up there."

She rolled her eyes. "He's such a prick. You should have seen him. He was holding court in the middle of the cafeteria today, all these kids hanging around him like he was a king or something. It was revolting."

"What about Taz?"

She shrugged her shoulders. "Would you come to school if your brother died?"

I lay down on my bed. "I don't think I can go back there."

"Where? To Tucker?"

Groaning at the word, I nodded.

She balled up a t-shirt and threw it at me. "Yeah, you can. You can't leave me there by myself."

I threw the shirt back at her and we sat in silence for few minutes. "Why would Cory lie about what happened?"

"We should go to SK*t. I heard the half-pipe is wicked."

I peered at her with a guilty smile. "Yeah, it is."

Anger flared in her face.

"Mom took me yesterday."

"Oh." She settled back into the chair looking smug. "That must have looked lame, walking in with your mom."

I sat up remembering Ev's offer. "One of the owners of Rox, not Mitch, the other guy, came up and gave me his card. I'm supposed to call him."

Tessa stared at me with her mouth open. "They want to sponsor you?"

I raised one shoulder in a shrug. "Maybe."

"Holy Shit! Ben! That's freaking amazing!" She threw her legs off the chair and leaned towards me. "Who cares about this shit with Cory?"

I stared at her, not trusting myself to speak. She met my eyes, the excitement drained from her face.

"I do. I care about the shit with Cory."

Her tough-girl façade couldn't hide her embarrassment.. "I know. I didn't mean it like that."

"A sponsorship won't make everything go away," I said quietly, not sure if she understood that I wasn't the same person I had been two days ago.

"I know," she said quickly. "But you can't lose this, Ben. This is your chance. Did you call him yet?"

"No."

"Do it now. I want to hear." She moved beside me on the bed and stared at me until I dialed the number. I got his voice mail.

"Hi, uh, Ev. This is Ben Olniuk. You gave me your card at SK*t yesterday. My cell number is 555-3459. Thanks. Bye."

Tessa tapped her foot impatiently. "Maybe you should text him?"

"You think?"

She shrugged. "He doesn't know your number, might not check his messages."

I chewed the inside of my mouth thinking. "Might look desperate. I'll wait 'til tomorrow. If he hasn't called back, I'll text him."

Ten minutes later, he did call back. Tessa leaned in so close to hear the conversation that one of her braids rested on my back.

"Hey, Ben. Mitch and I can meet you at the outdoor skatepark by the tracks at three o'clock tomorrow. Cool?" His voice had a drawl, like he was a California surfer, not a guy from Winnipeg.

"Yeah, that sounds awesome. See you then."

I shut my phone and took a deep breath.

"What if I suck?"

"As if. You never suck. I gotta go." Tessa grabbed her board and backpack. She paused at the door and turned around. "What about school on Monday?"

I shook my head. If kids at school thought Luke died because of me, it was the last place I wanted to be.

"Don't go on Facebook," she warned. With one hand on the door, she hesitated. "I wish you'd never gone with those guys." Her voice was quiet, and sad.

"Me too," I said and waved goodbye.

CORY

Two other girls waved at Michelle when Cory pulled up to the dance studio. *No money for new sneakers for me, but she can afford dance lessons for Michelle.* The bitter thoughts twisted Cory's face into a scowl. But, if he pointed out the unfairness, his mom would twist things around to make him look like a greedy asshole.

Cory's phone buzzed. It was another call from Kira. He let it go to voice mail. *She wants to talk about Luke.* The night already seemed far away and hazy, like a half-remembered dream.

Driving past a gas station, he heard someone holler his name. A group of guys wearing hoodies and baggie jeans leaned against an SUV. Swerving across a lane of traffic, Cory pulled in to the lot beside them. "Sweeeeet!" one of them whistled as they circled the car like a pack of wolves.

"Where'd you get the ride, bro?" His real name was Henry, but everyone called him Rico. He wore his hair greased back and flipped into a tail at the back.

Cory leaned his head out the window, but didn't get out, worried that Rico would slide into the front seat. "My dad's."

"I thought your dad was dead, bro? You still got his car?"

Passing a hand through his hair, Cory gave a wry laugh at his tactlessness. "Yeah, got the car, lost the dad. Sucks, eh?"

Rico stroked the hood of the car. "It's a sweet ride. How come you never bring it out?"

Cory honked the horn and Rico jumped. "Cuz guys like you molest it." Rico and the other two hooted.

"You should come party with us tonight." Cory knew who 'us' meant. Rico was in a gang called Warrior Nation.

Cory cocked his head at Rico as he considered the offer. It wasn't the first time a gang had courted Cory. He was charismatic and daring, a perfect combination in a gang member. Cory had always said no. He'd had Luke, Taz and Kira, and didn't need a gang. But things had changed.

Rico came to the driver side window and leaned in, his nicotine breath hot in Cory's face. Acne scars marked his skin and his hawk-like nose was so close that Cory could see dark hairs poking out of the nostrils. "Leland asked me about you. Thinks you might be a good fit. It's the house on Brewster, ten o'clock."

Rico swaggered back to his boys. Cory fired up the engine, gunned it a few times and peeled out of the lot. Getting asked to go to a Warrior Nation party was the first step. If they liked him, which he knew they would, they'd ask him to join.

Kira called again. This time he answered.

"Where are you? I've called you a million times!"

"Yeah, I got your messages."

She sounded irritated. "Why didn't you call me back?"

"I've got the car. I'll come get you. We can go for a drive."

She didn't answer right away, which pissed him off. He was about to tell her to forget it. "I'm not dressed yet," she said.

"Lazy Indian." Kira hated it when he made jokes like that.

"Screw you, Cory."

He laughed at her predictability. "I'll be there in fifteen minutes."

"Give me twenty," she yawned. Cory thought of Kira's long, tawny limbs stretching like a cat on her bed and grinned, clicking the phone shut.

When he pulled up to her house, she was sitting on the front steps. He watched as her spidery fingers twisted long strands of hair into a braid. Sitting down beside her, Cory squinted into the sun. "Hey," she whispered, abandoning the braid and letting it fall against her chest.

The Fall

"Hey," he whispered back. She leaned her head onto his shoulder. Tears slid down her cheek and fell on his shirt in dots of wetness. Cory felt her shudder. Instinctively, he wrapped an arm around her, pulling her against him. A lump formed in his throat, but he swallowed it away and concentrated on the feel of her body crushed against his. How long until she asked what happened to Luke? He steeled himself against the lies he'd have to tell her.

Maybe they weren't lies. In his head, Ben's guilt became more substantial, more real. He'd been the first one over the fence. He'd helped them get in. He'd been behind Luke when he'd started to cross the beam. Maybe he'd startled Luke, or even pushed him? He felt his chest get hot, hardening with anger. Ben needed to know there were repercussions. No one walks away unscathed when they watch someone die in front of them. No one.

He eyed a flowerbed across the street. It was surrounded by rocks—rocks that would send a message if they went through a window. Calmed at the thought of action, he cradled Kira's head against his chest and let her cry.

Saturday

BEN

My board careened over the uneven sidewalk. The sun felt good after a few days of self-inflicted solitary confinement.

    A bubble of excitement rose in my stomach when I got to the skatepark. Despite the spring weather, it was almost empty; only a few younger kids were goofing around at one end of the bowl. I wanted to get in a few practice runs before Ev and Mitch arrived. Strapping on my helmet and pads, I took a spin around the bowl to warm up, relaxing to the rhythm of my board against the pavement.

    I did a few ollies and grinds and then some tricks off the funbox in the middle of the bowl. My hair, wet now from sweat, curled around the edge of my helmet. I felt like a goldfish in a bowl when I realized how many kids had arrived while I'd been in Benjiland. I saw Tessa sauntering across the field and checked my phone. Almost three o'clock.

    The smirk she usually wore disappeared when she got to the edge of the bowl. In fact, she looked tense. Her eyes darted around the crowd. She must have been more nervous about how I'd do for Mitch and Ev than I thought.

The Fall

"What the hell is he doing here?" A guy's voice came from the other side. Tessa's braids swung violently against her shoulder as she turned to look at him. I saw her jaw clench and knew her eyes would be burning. All the chatter stopped and I froze in the middle of the bowl. He was talking about me.

"Luke would still be alive if it wasn't for you!" A girl hollered behind me.

More insults were hurled from above and someone threw an empty pop can at me. Tears sprang to my eyes and I blinked furiously to make them go away. I opened my mouth to shout the truth, but no sound came. Trapped and paralyzed, I waited for them to close in on me.

Tessa's voice shook me. She yelled my name again and I leaped across the bowl. Tossing my board beside her, I hauled myself up.

"Come on," Tessa said. "Let's get out of here."

The taunts followed us as we walked towards the road and ducked into a thicket of trees.

"Nobody followed us," Tessa said checking behind her. "Stoners aren't real energetic."

I sank to the ground and tried to make my hands stop shaking.

Tessa sat on her board beside me. "Are you okay?" Her braids hung down between her knees as she stabbed sticks into the ground.

"Ev and Mitch are going to think I bailed." I leaned back against a tree, its rough bark dug into my spine.

"Those kids can't stay there all day. Go back when no one's there."

Closing my eyes, I bit my lip to stop it from quivering. "What about at school? Does everyone think it's my fault?"

She was quiet so I knew I was right. I was a target. Going after me would turn into a game.

"You should talk to Cory. Tell him to straighten it out."

I narrowed my eyes at Tessa and raised my voice. "Talk to Cory? Are you kidding?"

"So what then, you're just going to sit here and let a sponsorship pass you by?" She met my eyes, her tone acidic.

I rolled my head against the tree, trying to make sense of everything.

Tessa was right, I couldn't lose a chance at a sponsorship, not when it was this close. Dialing Ev's number, I squeezed my eyes shut and waited for him to answer. "Ev? It's Ben. Hey, uh, I couldn't make it to the skatepark, something came up. I'm not trying to flake out or anything, but could we meet tomorrow?"

He said he'd talk to Mitch and call me back. Standing up, I wiped the leaves and mud off my jeans and picked up my board. "Let's go."

Tessa stabbed another stick into the ground, but didn't get up. "Grow a pair, Ben."

I rounded on her, my eyes wide. "What?"

"You heard me. Leave if you want, but I'm not following you."

Flashing a look full of bitterness and hurt, I turned and walked away. It wasn't possible to lose a sponsorship and my best friend in one day, was it?

The sound of the kids taunting me at the skatepark echoed in my ears. Even walking beside noisy traffic did nothing to drown it out.

I hated that I'd stood silent in the bowl. I could have spoken up against Cory's lies, but I'd just taken the abuse. What was wrong with me?

If only I'd left with Luke. It *had* been my fault, as much as anyone else's.

TAZ

Taz heard his dad leave for work, the door rattled against the metal frame as he slammed it. They hadn't spoken since the night at the hospital when he'd taken Taz's keys away. When they'd gotten home, he willingly surrendered the spare set, which his dad had taken without comment. Luke's death had added one more layer to the heavy cloud of hatred that had settled between them.

Coach had sent him a text that morning, asking if there was anything he needed. Even after all the shit that went down last year, Coach was still there for him. He hadn't texted anything back because he didn't know what to say. He needed his brother back, that was the first thing. And after that? More booze? Something to make the cancerous pain that was eating away at him go away.

His cell phone rang with a call from his dad. "The van's dead. You need to come get me."

No. You can rot in the parking lot waiting for me. "I don't have any keys, remember?"

His dad grunted. "I hid 'em behind my old trophies." He hung up.

His trophies. Typical. Taz sneered. The only fucking things he cared about, his stupid trophies. When he was a kid, he used sit with wide-eyed wonder gazing at the golden cups and medals that decorated a shelf in the basement. As he got older, the trophies lost their luster. He started to see his dad for what he was, a drunk who'd rather spend money on beer than his kids' school supplies. A guy who'd promise to take them for pancakes, but when morning came, be too hung over to get out of bed.

His dad knew he'd lost respect for him. It was why he'd shown up at the field last spring for the first football game, swerving into the parking lot with two loser friends. They'd yelled at the players, berating them. Taz felt his face burn as his dad and the other guys laughed when he fumbled the ball. Coach had started to walk over, but Taz caught his eye and waved him away. Jogging to the sidelines, Taz had taken off his helmet and met his dad, eye to eye. "Get outta here, Dad," he'd seethed. The cloud of bar smoke they'd been sitting in all afternoon clung to their clothes. His dad's face got red and his eyes bulged as the other two erupted into howls of laughter.

"Or what? You and your little friends gonna make me?" His dad sneered at Taz, "Never would have made it onto *my* team. You'll be lucky if you win a game."

A flood of aggression shot through Taz and he shoved him to the ground. His dad froze, laughter dying on his lips. "Take it back!" Taz yelled. He looked at his dad, lying on his back, and felt his anger rising. "You lying sack of shit. Take it back!" Their eyes locked. Even on the ground with his son towering over him, his father shook his head. Taz clenched his jaw. His dad was pushing him into a corner. "Take it back," he voice was hoarse and full of meaning.

His dad gave a twisted smile and whispered, "No."

A sick feeling grew in his stomach as he pulled his arm back to land a punch. A crowd of onlookers surrounded them, watching. "Go ahead, do it," his dad mocked. Taz crouched down, his fist pummeled his dad's stomach, a doughy mass. The contact was unrewarding. He went for the head, cracking his knuckles across his cheek. And then, grabbed the helmet lying beside him and smashed it down on his dad's forehead. The crack echoed across the field. His dad's hands flew to his head as blood gushed through them.

Someone had grabbed Taz from behind, hauling him off his dad. Enraged, he'd flung his arm around and caught Coach on the cheek with his helmet, splitting the skin.

The Fall

He didn't give the school a chance to kick him off the team. He'd quit that day and hadn't played ball since.

They'd never talked about what happened. Taz had no idea why his dad had shown up drunk that day, or why he'd acted like an ass. He buried the hurt with silence, erecting a wall between them, and started calling his dad Dennis. He'd crashed on Cory's bedroom floor for three weeks while his mom cajoled Dennis to let him back into the house, long enough for the gash across Dennis's forehead to heal into a bright pink scar. Since then, Taz and Dennis had stayed out of each other's way, agreeing to an uneasy truce for Luke and his mom. But that had ended with Luke's fall.

But, now his dad needed his help. He must have been desperate to call. Taz lay on his bed wondering what to do. He wanted the truck back, but the thought of spending even five minutes alone with the man made bile rise from his gut. He wished Dennis would come right out and blame him for Luke's fall. He wanted the chance to explain what happened, but doubted his dad would listen.

Dennis had gone back to work the day after Luke's fall. "Someone's got to pay for the goddamned funeral," he'd mumbled. Taz knew that wasn't the reason, he just didn't want to be around him or his mom.

Most of the time Taz's mom slept, but when she did come out of her room she'd shuffle through the house, suddenly burst into tears and then wander back to her room weeping. Luke always knew how to make her laugh, but Taz didn't. As much as he wanted to say the right thing, he'd stand mute as she walked past him.

Taz could hear her hiccupping sobs as he lay on his bed. He dragged himself up and went to find the keys to his truck. They were tucked behind the cup from Tucker High 1984. A dusty picture of the football team sat beside it; boys with long, feathered hair wearing yellow and blue jerseys, their helmets tucked under their arms, stood in a line in front of the school. Taz tipped the trophy cup and spat in it, adding to the large wad of dried spit that already sat in the bottom.

When he put the keys in the ignition, the engine gave a sputtery, choking wheeze as he reversed out of the driveway.

His dad's back was to him when he pulled into the parking lot. He'd popped the hood on the mini-van and leaned over the engine, a crack of pasty flesh showed between his pants and shirt. He looked like any flabby, middle-aged man who worked a crappy job for no money. Who would believe he'd once been a football player?

Taz parked beside him and Dennis spoke without looking up. "I think the fan belt went. I'll get Joe's to tow it in. You got any cash on you?" He lit a cigarette. The flame caught the tip and flared with an orange glow.

"No."

He sighed as if Taz had purposefully not brought any to annoy him.

"I'll have to write a cheque and hope it don't bounce." Pulling the bar that held up the hood, he let it slam down and climbed in the passenger side of the truck. His cigarette dangled out the side of his mouth. When Luke and he were kids they used to copy their father, trying to balance a smoke on their lips, as they talked to each other. Every time Luke's fell out, he'd yelp and hop around like it had burned off his dick.

"You lined up any work for summer yet?" He rolled down the window and flicked some ash off the end of his cigarette. Taz caught a glimpse of his own eyes in the rearview mirror. The hardness in them surprised him. They looked like his dad's.

The Fall

He shrugged. It was only April, but he knew that if he wanted to run his lawn care business again, he should have called some clients from last year and put leaflets in mailboxes by now. All the enthusiasm about starting it up again had disappeared. He couldn't keep two thoughts in his head since Luke's fall. His dad grunted and a smirk crept across his face. "You're graduating soon. Time to start paying rent, or move out."

"That what you want? Me to move out?" Taz took the bait. Luke would have laughed it off, but Taz couldn't.

Dennis took a long, slow puff of his cigarette and exhaled a dragon-like plume of smoke. "By the time I was your age I was living on my own. Supporting myself. If I didn't have money for beer, I didn't eat." He snorted at his joke. Resettling in the seat, the springs squeaked under his dad's weight. "You think you can sit in the basement forever? I'll kick your lazy ass out." Taz could feel his dad's stare, judging if he was ready for the fight.

They were almost home and a half full bottle of vodka lay under Taz's bed. He'd found it that afternoon in Luke's drawer.

"Luke wasn't going to sit around doing nothing. That boy had initiative. Remember when he sold your bike, but told you it had been stolen? He used the money to buy a new one and sold his old one to you?" He chuckled at the memory and passed a hand through his thinning hair.

"That was me, Dad. I sold his bike. Luke was too stupid to figure it out."

Dennis closed his eyes and tensed his shoulders. "Don't you talk about your brother that way," he growled.

"Luke was Luke. I knew who he was," Taz said evenly.

"And I didn't?" The words were an accusation.

"You aren't remembering him like you did."

"I knew my own kid!" he yelled.

"Bullshit! Stop acting like he was perfect," Taz yelled back. Blood throbbed through his body. He wanted to hit something.

"He's not here to set the record straight, is he?" The silent accusation burned in his eyes, smoldering like a cigarette. It had hung between them since he'd picked Taz up from the hospital.

"It wasn't my fault he fell."

His dad snorted and shook his head. "Always the coward. Too afraid to take the blame. You just go on blaming your brother then."

Fury took hold of Taz. He wanted to drive into a lamppost, even if it totaled the truck, it would be worth it to see blood gush from his dad's head. He'd made it across the beam, twice. He hadn't lost his balance. His dad could have lost two sons that night, instead of just one.

"Stop the goddamned truck!" Dennis shouted. Taz had driven past the house. His dad's fist slammed into the dash and Taz hit the brakes. Flying forward, Dennis caught himself and jumped out before Taz reversed. He ran across the neighbour's yard and into the house, the fat of his stomach jiggling. If Taz hadn't been shaking with rage, he might have found it funny.

BEN

When I got home, my phone buzzed with a text from Ev. "Tmw no good. Tuesday @ 2 pm @ SK*t?" I sighed with relief. They still wanted to see me. At least in the middle of the afternoon at Sk*t there was less chance of running into kids from Tucker.

With the night dragging on, I decided to watch some skate boarding videos on the computer. My Facebook page popped up and without thinking, I logged on. A stream of posts to my wall came up:

The Fall

"I wish I'd been up there too. I would have pushed you off myself."

"You're a fucking loser."

"Don't show your face at Tucker again."

Staring at the screen, I couldn't believe the words were directed at me. A hot flush spread up from the base of my neck, engulfing my head. People *hated* me because of Cory's lies. How could I stand up for myself when it was me against everyone?

I wanted to throw the computer, toss it around the room and smash it. Holding my head in my hands, I wondered if there was anything I could post to tell my side of the story. But, with my eyes closed, all that flashed through my mind was Luke asking to leave with me.

I was still awake when Mom got home from her night shift. "Can't sleep?" she asked leaning against the doorframe. She rubbed her eyes and stifled a yawn.

"No," I said and turning over to look at her.

"How was your audition?" I felt the weight of the bed shift as she sat down.

I rolled my eyes at her choice of words, "Didn't happen."

"Why not?"

I choked on the truth. "It's rescheduled for Tuesday."

There was a crash in the living room. We both jumped up. "What was that?" I asked, tossing off the cover and bolting from my room.

Chilly night air blew in from the hole where our window used to be. Mom turned on the lights. A rock the size of my head lay in front of the couch.

Mom stared at the rock and the window with wide eyes. My heart started to hammer in my chest. "Shit!" Mom swore. We both froze in the middle of the living room. Mom moved first, spinning around shaking glass out of pillows and moving furniture out of the way. Then stopped and pressed her hands to her forehead as if trying to calm down. She took a deep breath. "Go put some shoes on," she ordered. "And find some cardboard boxes in the basement. We need to get this window covered."

I went to the basement looking for a piece of cardboard big enough to tape over the hole. The first box was too small, so I tossed it out of the way. Then, I grabbed another one and threw it with more force. It hit the wall and bounced off. Pent up frustration exploded out of me and I stomped the boxes, kicking and throwing them around the basement.

After reading the posts on Facebook, I knew a rock coming through my living room window hadn't been random. Had Cory thrown the rock? Or had someone else because of his lies?

The vacuum roared, bits of glass crackling through the hose as Mom ran it over the carpet with frenzied energy. I stood watching her, wondering if I should tell her about the skatepark and posts on Facebook. She'd freak out. I couldn't do that to her. It was my problem. I had to figure out how to handle it.

I picked up the rock. Pitted with jagged edges, it was heavy. Mom held the door for me as I backed outside with it and heaved it into the bushes. A cop car stopped in front of the house and two officers stepped out. I could hear static and a fuzzy voice on the radio as they slammed the car doors. One turned on a flashlight and shone it at the front window and at the stubby grass below.

"Hi there." He was older, with silvery hair and a thick mustache. "We had a call from a neighbour." I squinted when he turned the flashlight to my face.

"Someone threw a rock through our window." I pointed to it, lying half covered by a bush.

The Fall

Mom looked relieved to see the cops. They introduced themselves and asked what happened. "I just got home from work and we heard a crash." She gestured to the window. "We found the rock sitting on our living room floor."

I looked around, across the street, Mr. DePaulo's front window glowed yellow behind the curtains.

"Any idea who might have done this?" The younger officer looked pointedly at me.

I stared at my feet and shook my head.

"Ben?" Mom's tone made me look at her. "If you think you know, say something."

As if it was that easy. What if I did accuse Cory? It wouldn't help anything, in fact, it would make things worse. I shook my head again.

"Did you see anyone?" The cop asked.

Mom and I shook our heads. "We were in the back of the house."

"All right," tucking the notepad back in his pocket, he gave the house a final appraisal. "We'll go talk to the witness. Here's our card," he passed it to Mom. "and that," he pointed to a number at the top, "is the incident report number. Call us if there's anything else."

They walked down the sidewalk and crossed the street. Mr. DePaulo opened the door and they disappeared inside.

CORY

The Warrior Nation clubhouse on Brewster St. had seen better days. Rusty bed rails, old tools and a toilet bowl littered the yard. White paint peeled off the wood siding and a screen door hanging off its hinges squeaked when the wind blew.

Cory parked the corvette on the street. No one would be stupid enough to pull anything on a car in front of the Warrior Nation clubhouse. He'd searched the house for half an hour before he had found the keys, hidden again in a box of wedding photographs in his mom's room, and pocketed them.

Before he could knock, Rico opened the door. He wasn't wearing a shirt and Cory's gaze landed on the Warrior Nation tattoo over his heart. The grinning skull wore a feather headdress and clutched a dagger between its teeth. "Hey, bro!" He clapped Cory on the shoulder and led him into a dining room that stank of dried piss and beer. It was hot and airless and five other shirtless guys sat around a card table. Crooked blinds covered the windows and rock music thudded from a stereo. All conversation stopped when Cory entered the room.

Leland sat at the head of the table on a lawn chair. He motioned for Cory to sit on a crate across the table from him. "We were just talking about you." Leland's voice was hoarse, like he'd been up all night yelling at a concert. His long hair, pulled back into a ponytail, was jet black. Tattoos covered his chest and arms, most of them swirling tribal markings that ended in sharp points. A halo of space surrounded the Warrior Nation tattoo on his chest.

Leland introduced the other guys. Besides Rico and Leland's right hand man, Johnny, there was Happy, who already looked stoned, Dustin and Franklin. Neither of the last two had Warrior Nation tattoos. Leland told Dustin to get him and Cory a beer each. Dustin reached into the cooler beside the table and shook the ice off a bottle, cracked the cap off and handed it to Cory. Tilting it to Leland, Cory took a chug. The liquid felt thick as it slid down his throat.

"Sorry about your friend. Rico told me you were tight with him."

Cory wiped his mouth and nodded.

"We all know what it's like to lose a brother." The other guys murmured their agreement. "We lost one of our own recently." Leland drew a cigarette out of a box on the table and tapped the filter end on the back. Dustin dug a lighter out of his jeans pocket, bent forward and held the flame for Leland. After it caught, he leaned back and exhaled a column of smoke. It swirled around the bare bulb hanging from the ceiling. Sitting on a lawn chair, with one leg crossed over the other and a cigarette in his hand, he reminded Cory of his dad relaxing in the backyard.

"We could use you, Cory." Leland stared at him and blew more smoke up to the ceiling. "You interested?" He flicked some ash into a can of beer and waited for Cory to speak.

He felt the weight of five pairs of eyes on him. He'd ignored their interest before, but this time it felt right. "Yeah, I am." Cory's voice sounded deeper, more masculine than he remembered. As if in that one response, he'd aged ten years.

A slow, steady smile spread across Leland's face. "Looks like we got a new chubby, boys."

Fetching beers and lighting cigarettes wasn't Cory's thing, but he didn't plan on being on the bottom of the totem pole for long. He cast a sideways glance at Dustin who stared at Cory with open hostility.

More beer cans hissed open and the music got louder. Cory started to move his head to the beat of the song and shared a laugh with Johnny. He liked hanging out with these guys. It was the first time he didn't feel the weight of Luke's death hanging over him. Being around them, and free of his past, meant he could reinvent himself.

The room had gotten hotter. Leland sat down beside Cory. Dark stubble grew in patches along his jawline and on his upper lip. Still shirtless, tufts of curly hair poked out of his armpits as he rested his arms on his knees. "We're gonna need more beer. You ready to go get it?"

Cory knew he wasn't going to pay for it. The beer buzz wore off immediately.

"Dustin's going with you." Dustin's head jerked up at the sound of his name, like a trained dog.

"I don't need help," Cory said and met Leland's eyes. He didn't like Dustin's shifty gaze or the way he sat silently on a crate in the corner.

Leland smirked. "He's not help, he's keeping you honest, making sure you don't cheat."

Cory's phone rang as soon as he and Dustin got in the car. The caller ID said it was Kira. He debated taking it, but knew if he didn't, she'd keep calling. "Yeah?" he answered.

"Cory?"

"I'm in the middle of something."

"In the middle of what?"

"Stuff," he glanced at Dustin. "What do you want?"

"I just wanted to see you." Her voice got thick.

Don't make me be an asshole to you. She started to say something else, but he cut her off "I gotta go. I'll call you later." And snapped the phone shut.

Thinking about Kira was going to make him lose focus. He took a deep breath and cracked his neck. He'd stolen stuff before, not because he had to, for the adrenaline rush.

The parking lot was empty. There were two guys leaning against each other on a bench across the street, but they looked too drunk to notice anything. Cory sat in the car watching the guy working at the counter, a skinny Asian with hair that stood in shiny spikes.

The Fall

"You gonna do this, or what?" Dustin asked. Cory shot him a look and pulled his ball cap lower.

"You wanna screw off? I'm going." He left the car running and hauled the liquor store door open. A chime rang. The guy at the counter looked at him without expression. Cory walked to the fridge at the back and kept his head down. He grabbed two six-packs of beers, and stuck one under his arm. With his free hand, he grabbed a huge bottle of beer, the glass cold and hard in his hand and walked to the counter. The man's eyes flicked from Cory to the beer.

"You got ID?" he asked.

"Yeah," Cory reached into his back pocket and came up empty. "Oh, shit. I left it in the car." As he turned towards the door, he tossed the beer bottle off the counter. It smashed on the floor in a foamy flood at the man's feet. Cory grabbed a six-pack of beer in each hand and raced out the door. The cans dangled at odd angles and he dropped one as he kicked the door open with his foot. Dustin had moved to the driver side and started to reverse when Cory jumped in, the beer cans knocking together. The car door wasn't shut before the corvette squealed out of the parking lot.

TAZ

Taz had been driving aimlessly for hours. It was after midnight when he drove past the movie theatre and parked at the construction site. Other than ripped yellow police tape hanging off the chain link fence like streamers, it looked the same as before. He wondered if the ground was still stained with Luke's blood.

He twisted off the cap of a bottle of vodka, left over from a night at Garbage Hill. The clear glass bottle glinted in the darkness as he brought it to his mouth. The alcohol hit his empty stomach with a thud.

The vodka didn't last long. After swirling the last few drops in the bottle and tipping them into his mouth, he opened the car door, stepped out and hurled the bottle against a steel post. His aim was perfect and the glass shattered and flew in all directions, littering the site with jagged shrapnel. He got back in the truck and reversed. The thought of going home to see his dad turned his stomach, but there was nowhere else to go. How much longer could they live like this, with his dad punishing him? Did it take away some of his hurt, to make Taz suffer?

As he turned onto a street close to his house, he watched a girl with long hair and a small, perfectly curved ass walking. It was Kira Grayeyes. He honked and she spun around with her hand over her chest.

"Christ, Taz! You scared the shit out of me!" Her eyes widened in surprise.

"Get in."

She hesitated, looking down the street. "Yeah? I hate walking alone at night."

He leaned across the seat, the vinyl creaking, to unlock the door for her. He held out a hand to help her climb from the curb into the truck. "You haven't been at school," she said as she clicked the buckle into place.

"Yeah, my brother died."

She closed her eyes at the blunt words and bit her lip. "I—" she stammered. "I was going to call. To see how you were doing."

"I'm shitty, thanks for asking. And you?" He was trying to be funny, but as she shrunk away in the seat he regretted his callous words.

"I don't know."

"What do you mean, you don't know? Everyone knows how they're doing." He rested one elbow against the window glass and kept the other one on the top of the steering wheel.

"I feel like I woke up in someone else's life. Everything feels different."

He bit back another smart-ass comment. "Yeah, I know what you mean."

They sat quietly for a few blocks. He watched Kira's shadow appear on the dash each time they drove under a streetlight. "Have you seen Cory?" She asked quietly.

He shook his head. "You?"

She shrugged. "For like five minutes," she grumbled. "I wish he'd tell me what happened. I hate wondering."

Taz gritted his teeth.

"Oh God, I'm sorry. I didn't mean—" She stumbled over her apology, bringing her hands to her face. "Was it Cory's fault?" She whispered the question and shrunk back in her seat waiting for the answer.

"No."

"He made it seem like it was that skater's fault. Everyone's blaming him."

"Shit." Taz groaned and rubbed a hand through his hair. He'd forgotten Ben had even been there. "It wasn't his fault."

Taz pulled up to Kira's house. "You can call me, you know, if you need anything." She said, her eyes downcast, then flickering up to his face. "Thanks for the ride." She hopped out of the truck and walked to her front door.

He sat in the truck for a few minutes, not ready to drive away. He didn't know what kids were saying about Luke, or the night he fell, and he didn't care. But, it wasn't right that Cory was blaming Ben, Luke would have been pissed. Luke had done crazy things, but never to hurt anyone else. Taz had been the one who'd gotten off on finding targets to bully, not Luke. Luke had been the good one. It shouldn't have been Luke who fell, good guys were supposed to live. And bad guys fall.

Out of nowhere, tears filled his eyes and rolled down his cheeks, the first ones since Luke's fall.

CORY

Cory leaned his head back and yelped with relief.

"Bro, you tore out of there like it was on fire!"

"Did he come after me? Did you see?" Cory asked breathlessly and looked in the mirror. "I knocked a bottle of beer over behind the counter," he explained laughing. "Then, grabbed the six packs."

Dustin changed the radio to a rap station as he drove.

"What the hell is this?" Cory said, turning it back to the classic rock station. "You're not driving some pimped out Cadillac Escalade!"

"I like that music." The chippy tone in his voice didn't match the wary glance he gave Cory.

"Not in my car."

Dustin slammed the brakes hard in front of the house and Cory jerked forward. Cory swore at him and snatched the keys out of the ignition. "Lock your door," he shouted over his shoulder.

Leland and the others didn't look up from their poker game when Cory walked in. "Put the beers in the fridge, chubby," Rico said before folding.

A blast of cool air hit Cory when he opened the fridge door and found ten other six-packs, all ice cold and waiting to be drunk. He heard Rico's distinctive nasal laugh and slammed the door shut. All of them were in hysterics, especially Dustin who had walked in behind Cory. He mimicked Cory's panicked exit of the store to louder laughter. Cory's nostrils flared and he clenched his fists. He hated being made a fool, especially when a guy like Dustin was in on it. But, he couldn't storm out of the house, not if he wanted to be part of Warrior Nation. He swung at Rico catching him on the arm. "You bastards!"

Leland clapped a hand on his shoulder. "Get yourself a beer," he said nodding towards the kitchen.

Rico sidled up to Cory, "Hey, bro. Can you drop me at my girlfriend's place? She lives on Maplewood."

"I'm your taxi service now?" Cory asked trying to keep the tone light.

Rico didn't find it funny. "Yeah, bro, you are. You're the chubby, remember?"

"I was heading out anyway. You ready now?"

Leland hadn't moved from his spot at the card table and his pile of winnings had grown. Cory wondered if the guys let him win, or he was that good. Rico went to say goodbye and Leland leaned over and whispered something. They both looked at Cory. He met their gazes.

"Leland likes you," Rico said as he got out of Cory's car. A thick curl of dark hair had sprung loose and hung down his forehead. "Thinks you're a good fit."

Cory gave an indifferent grunt.

"We'll be in touch." He held out his hand for a fist bump and walked up the sidewalk. The leather seat held the indentation of his body as Cory drove down the block. He was close to Kira's house. She'd slam the door in his face if she knew he'd been hanging out with the Warriors.

He texted her. "R u awake?"

"No."

"I miss you." He knew how to play her. Open up a little and she'd come back to him.

"No you don't."

"I do. Meet me outside."

"Why?"

"Please?"

"Ok"

Grinning, he turned the car around and drove to her place. The curtain in the front window waved a minute after Cory pulled up. Kira yelled something to whoever was inside and walked to the car. She was in a pair of Cory's old sweats and a t-shirt that left most of her flat stomach bare. Her hair waved behind her as she ran to the car.

He rolled down the window. "Wanna go for a—" but she cut him off.

"Why did you tell people it was Ben's fault?" Kira narrowed her eyes, waiting for him to speak. The directness of her question caught him off-guard. "Are you going to answer me?"

Cory snorted, like the answer didn't matter. "Why do you care?" Anger started to brew in him.

"The whole school hates him! You should see what's written on his locker."

"So? He was there. Maybe it was his idea, I don't know. My best friend died that night, that's all I remember."

She rolled her eyes, "Since when was Luke your best friend?"

"I've known him as long as I've known Taz. They were like brothers to me."

"Like brothers? Have you even seen Taz since Luke died?"

The words rang in Cory's ears. He didn't want to see Taz. It would only remind him of what had happened.

Kira's disgust showed in her eyes and the tightness in her mouth. He couldn't look at her. "I got new friends now."

"What's that supposed to mean?"

He paused. Once she knew about the gang, it was over. But watching her stand in the street, scolding him with her hands on her hips, he wanted her to know what he'd chosen. "Warrior Nation. I'm not screwing around with a bunch of losers anymore." Kira stepped back from the car, eyes wide with shock.

Before she could say anything, he put the car in drive and pulled past her into the street. She stood in the middle of the road staring after him.

It wasn't until Cory was halfway back to his house that he wondered who had told her what had happened the night Luke fell.

Elmer's car was parked in the driveway blocking the corvette's spot in the garage. He didn't want to leave the vette outside overnight. Grabbing a set of his mom's keys from the house, he moved her car out of the garage and pulled the corvette into her spot.

Cory wondered how much his mom had told Elmer about his dad. Did it occur to him that he was sleeping in the same bed where his dad had once slept? The dip in the mattress where his fat ass lay had been made by another man whose children slept a few feet away.

A sudden, uncontrollable rush of anger flooded through his body. It hammered in his ears. He grabbed a baseball bat leaning against the wall of the garage and swung it wildly. It took a few hits to break the windshield glass on her car. With each whack, he felt the glass give a little, until it exploded in a shower of perfectly formed cubes that sprayed across the driveway. He stood holding the bat and panting. He tossed the bat into the garage and it rolled under his dad's car. He left it there.

TAZ

The ashtray on the kitchen table overflowed with gray ash and crumpled butts. Taz's mom sat in her bathrobe and slippers, a cigarette dangling from her fingers.

Taz eyed her warily. "Why are you still up?"

She stubbed her cigarette out and the whole pile threatened to spill. "I wanted to talk to you." She kept her voice low and nodded to the living room. His dad lay snoring in the recliner. Crushed beer cans littered the floor around him.

"I've never seen him so angry, Taz. It was all I could do to keep him from changing the locks." His mom's voice trembled and her jowls shook like a turkey's neck. Usually an obnoxious drunk, his dad had never laid a hand on his mom, but sometimes Taz wished he would, then he'd have an excuse to do worse than crack his forehead with a helmet.

"Why's he so angry with me? He started the fight." Cracking his knuckles, Taz glared at his father's bulk, sleeping soundly in the corner. "He thinks Luke's fall was my fault."

His mom reached for another cigarette, but stopped herself. Her hands shook, from nicotine or emotion, Taz didn't know. "Yeah," she said quietly.

"Do you?"

She shook her head, but didn't look at him. Her lip quivered and tears started to drop on her bathrobe, disappearing in the thick terry cloth fabric. "Maybe you should stay at a friend's house for a few days. Until he cools off." She put her elbows on the table and pressed her fingertips against her temples.

Taz's insides churned with disgust. His dad's arms hung limply beside the chair; his slackened mouth widening with each inhalation. Taz closed his eyes against the image of himself passed out on Garbage Hill. Would he be this old, fat drunk one day too?

"It was an accident! You think I wouldn't have stopped it if I could?"

She nodded as her body shook with sobs.

"Tell him I'll be gone by tomorrow." Taz slammed the cheap metal chair against the table and thundered down the stairs. He dug out the bottle hidden under his mattress and held it in his hands. With a few swallows, the evening would fade into a blur and he'd pass out.

But, he needed a clear head to get a job and find a place to crash.

Stuffing the bottle in a drawer, he flopped on his bed, the familiar tang of sweat clung to the sheets.

He couldn't go on like this. Without Luke, his family was falling apart.

He dreamt that night that he was playing football against a whole team of Lukes, their faces pulpy messes. His dad stood on the sidelines bellowing that he was a coward. The Lukes advanced on Taz, but he couldn't move. His legs had morphed into lifeless stumps rooted to the ground.

When he woke up the next morning, his throat was hoarse from calling out.

Taz made some calls, leaving messages with anyone he knew who could get him some work. It was mid-afternoon and his dad would be home soon. Finally, Russ, a Garbage Hill regular who ran a window washing business called him back.

"Hey, man. I'm looking for some work. You got anything?"

Russ's voice was deep and thick, like he'd been punched in the face a few times. "Like on weekends?" The phone line crackled with wind and Taz imagined Russ on a scaffold high up on a building, his feet hanging off the ledge as he spoke with him.

"Nah, I need something now, like right away. Had a fight with my dad. I need a place to crash too."

"Shit," he heard Russ exhale. "Yeah, I can make something work. You wanna stay at my place for a few days? All I got is a couch."

Taz felt the knot in his stomach loosen. How could a guy he'd only met a few months ago treat him better than his own family? "Thanks, man."

Grabbing an old hockey bag, he stuffed it with some clean blankets and his pillow. He took some beer from the fridge, reveling in the thought of Dad coming home from work, opening the fridge and finding the shelf empty.

Taz dumped his bag in the back of the truck and reversed out of the driveway. He drove slowly past the house. Peeling paint, crooked front steps and a fence whose pickets barely clung together. There was no reason for him to ever go back there. Without Luke, his family was falling apart.

Sunday

BEN

Mom had already left for work when I woke up, but her name flashed on my phone as I slapped peanut butter on my toast. "How are you feeling?" she asked. I could hear people talking in the background. She must have been at the nurse station in the middle of the ward.

"I'm okay," I lied. After last night, neither one of us had slept much. I worried that a rock through our window was only a warning.

"Mama called me and wondered if you'd go by the restaurant today after the lunch rush and help Papa with the chairs." She paused. "I thought it might be a good idea." Her voice trailed off. I knew she wanted someone to babysit me. "And, one other thing," she cleared her throat and lowered her voice. "The funeral is Tuesday at two o'clock at St. Thomas, I just read it in the paper. I think we should go. Or, at least you should go. I'll try my best to get someone to cover my shift."

"What?" I pushed the toast away, no longer hungry. "I can't go to Luke's funeral." How could I show my face there? If she knew what people said on Facebook, she'd never have suggested it.

She cut me off before I could say more. "Why not? He was your friend too."

Resting my butt against the edge of the counter, I felt the hot flush of tears prickle behind my eyes. "I can't go by myself." My voice wavered.

"Okay," she sighed. "Can you ask Tessa? Or your dad?"

"Dad? Are you kidding?" I asked, shocked that she suggested it.

"I called him this morning," she admitted. "After last night ... he's going to come by today to check on you."

"I don't need anyone to check on me, especially not him." Anger settled in my stomach like a stone. *Now* he wants to be a father?

"He's your dad, Ben. He needs to know what's going on." She said it calmly, but her voice had an edge to it. Like a cat hissing a warning.

I snorted. "When it suits you."

"What's that supposed to mean?" she whispered angrily into the phone.

"Nothing."

"I have to get back to work, my break's almost over. I called the insurance company before I left for work. The deductible will be $150."

Mom only mentioned money when she wanted me to pay for something. "I didn't throw the stupid rock, why do we have to pay for it?"

"That's how it works." She sounded resigned, one more shitty thing she had to deal with. "It'd be nice if your dad chipped in for things like this," she muttered and then took a deep breath, her exhalation heavy in my ear. "We'll talk about it later. I'm working late tonight."

I'd forgotten about helping out Mama and Papa, but being at the restaurant was better than being trapped at home. The lunch rush wouldn't be over for another hour, so I dropped onto the couch and turned on the TV. My mood lifted a little when I saw that one of the sports channels had a skate boarding competition on. World class guys nailed tricks and skated flawlessly. I knew I could be as good as them. They were a couple of years older than me, but they'd started out just like me, finding a local sponsor and entering competitions.

My stomach plummeted when I remembered that I was supposed to meet Ev and Mitch on Tuesday. At the same time as the funeral.

I had to change our meeting time again. My hands got sweaty dialing Ev's number.

"Ev's phone."

"Hey, uh, is Ev there?"

"Nope. Who's this?" I could hear a machine grinding metal in the back and music blaring.

"It's Ben Olniuk. Ev's supposed to see me skate on Tuesday."

"Hey." His voice got friendlier. "It's Mitch. What's up?"

I took a deep breath. "I have to go to a funeral on Tuesday afternoon. Could we get together in the morning instead? Or later, after it's over?"

"Yeah, yeah, dude. Whatever. I'll have Ev call you to set it up. Later." He hung up. Would the message get to Ev? Staring at the cardboard window, I wondered what could make this day suck more?

The doorbell rang. A man in navy blue overalls and work boots shuffled on the front steps. Dad. I opened the wooden door, but kept the screen door shut. A worn cap on his head said "Parkham Industries."

"Hiya, Ben. Thought I'd come by and see how you were doing." When he smiled the silver cap on his front tooth gleamed.

I eyed him warily. "I'm okay." Mom had told him to come by, but he made it sound like it was his idea.

"Can I come in for a minute?" He adjusted the cap on his head and shuffled side to side.

I unlocked the screen door. He smelled like oil and grit. Smudges of grease shone on his face and rims of black edged his fingernails.

"So, uh, your mom told me your friend's funeral is on Tuesday. Thought I'd go with you."

I didn't say anything. He'd been AWOL for the last eight years and now he wants to come to a funeral?

"Tessa's going with me," I lied.

He grinned, the tooth shining. "That your girlfriend?"

"No," I snapped. "She's been my best friend for like four years," I added, not bothering to hide my annoyance.

"I'd still like to go, you know, to support you." He took off his hat and ran a hand through his hair.

"I know Mom told you to go to the funeral. You don't have to." Better to give him the out now, than have him bail on Tuesday.

Jim's face sagged. As if all the effort he'd put into holding it up had exhausted him and he let go. "Well, yeah, that's part of it." He paused, rolling the rim of his cap in his hands. "Hearing about that friend of yours, it got me thinking. It could have been you up there. I could be going to your funeral." He paused and put his cap back on, pulling it low over his eyes. "And I barely know you."

I met his eyes, and for once, didn't look away first. "It starts at two o'clock."

Dad gave me a slow grin and nodded. "Alright, then." With a low whistle, he peeked around the corner and looked at the cardboard covering the window. "Your mom told me about that." As if he and Mom were buddies.

The Fall

He dug into the back pocket of his overalls. "Give this to your mom, will ya?" It was an envelope thick with $20 bills. "It's for the window."

I watched from the door as he drove his beater down the street. I wondered what Mom would say when she saw the cash. Sometimes, it made her angry when he tried to help, like he was saying she couldn't do it on her own. And other times she railed against him for never helping.

More than anything, I wanted to talk to Tessa. She'd flip when I told her Dad was going to the funeral. Actually, she'd flip when she found out I was going to the funeral. The thought of walking into a church filled with Luke's friends and family scared the crap out of me. I didn't know if I could go through with it without her.

"I'm goin 2 Luke's funeral" I texted her. And added, "With Jim." That would get her attention.

It only took a few minutes before she responded. "20 bux says he doesn't sho"

"R u comin?"

"r u serious?"

"Please. Jim might bail. I can't go alone."

I held my breath and waited for her response. But, it didn't come.

Papa looked up from a soccer game on TV when I knocked on the front door, rattling the glass. Closed after the lunch rush, they'd re-open around five o'clock and took the afternoon break to clean up and prep for dinner. At least Mama did. Papa spent most of the afternoon watching European soccer on satellite TV.

With a wet kiss on both cheeks, he brought me into the restaurant. Lemony fried potatoes and whatever spices they use on the meat skewers filled the air. He reached up to wrap an arm around my neck, showing me what he wanted me to do. "We change the chairs. Mama want new seats," he said in heavily accented English.

Mama burst from the back when she heard my voice, carrying an armload of folded vinyl. "My Benny! You want eat now?" She planted more kisses on my cheeks and dropped the vinyl on the table. "Patti bring gun of staples," she winked at me. "She say you forget."

I laughed and shook my head. Of course, I had forgotten. I wasn't hungry, but I knew better than to say that to Mama, whose mission in life was to feed me til I burst. "I'll eat later, after the chairs are finished."

"Okay, you and Papa work. I make souvlaki for special tonight."

The soccer game stayed on and Papa groaned and yelled at the TV in Greek while Mama chopped and fried onions, banging pans in the kitchen. Papa unscrewed the legs on the chairs while I cut vinyl for new seat covers and stapled it on. We worked quietly, each of us involved with our task until Papa spoke. "Patti tell me about the troubles." He shook his head, "I no happy to hear. You okay?"

Papa looked at me, skin folded over his eyes and his bushy brows knit together. "I could have left before we climbed. I keep wondering what would have happened if I had. Maybe he wouldn't have fallen." The staple gun snapped, kicking back as it fired into the bottom of the seat.

"Aiyiyi," Papa muttered He screwed legs back to the seat and flipped up our first chair. Papa looked at me, running his stubby fingers against the gray bristles on his beard. "In Greece, I got one brother, Theo. Long time, my family save up money, but finally only enough to send one boy to Canada. I say goodbye to my family. I go. Theo die after I leave. I no find out til many months later." Papa grew quiet and watched the TV. Even when the other team scored a goal, he didn't react. "I always wonder. What if I no come? If Theo come to Canada, maybe he no die."

Papa had never told me about his brother. "It wasn't your fault, Papa."

He gave me a sad smile. "It happen long time ago when I a young man. But it still make me sad, you know. This trouble stay with you for a long time, but it no your fault, Benny. You a good boy."

His words seeped into me. I tried to put another staple in, but tears made my eyes too blurry to see. His warm, weathered hand clamped on my shoulder. "You a good boy."

I nodded, so he'd know I heard him, not because I agreed. A good boy would have taken Luke away, told him not to cross the beam, that following Cory was a stupid idea. Instead, I'd stood silent, like I always did.

When we'd finished the chairs and Mama had inspected them, she went to pack up some souvlaki and rice for Mom, and a piece of baklava for me. "You take garbage?" Papa asked me. He held the door while I tossed boxes and bags into the alley dumpster. A car, its motor loud in the empty alley drove toward us. Glancing into the car, I saw the driver wore a bandana and sunglasses; gang members. I looked away, but a familiar face riding shotgun stared back at me and my eyes grew wide.

Cory.

He smirked at me through the open window, twisting in his seat to keep his eyes locked on mine as he drove past. A sick feeling started in the pit of my stomach and worked its way up my throat. Pulling the door shut behind me, I realized my hands were shaking.

"Benny?" Papa called from the front of the restaurant. The ding of the register sounded. "Here, Benny. You work hard today,"

Papa said handing $20 to me. I felt guilty taking money from him, but tucked the bill into my pocket anyway, and took the paper bag of food from Mama. They waved at me through the front window as I hopped on my board, glancing down the street for Cory's car. It was driving in the opposite direction of my house, a few blocks down. Get home fast, I told myself.

At the corner, I had to wait for traffic. Cars whizzed past, the smell of exhaust floating around me. A group of kids were waiting on the corner across the street, laughing and talking. I recognized a few of them from Tucker, a couple used to hang out at the skatepark. I felt self-conscious. They'd probably heard rumours about me, or read things on Facebook. I wasn't anonymous anymore. Pulling my hat down low over my eyes, I dropped my board and rushed to skate down a few blocks before going to their side of the street, a car screeched to a stop, narrowly missing me. The driver leaned out his window and yelled. "Crazy skater! Watch where you're going!"

A few seconds later I heard the kids shouting. "That's him! That's the kid who pushed Luke!" Traffic was too heavy for them to cross. I picked up my board and took off, hoping to lose them before it let up. Honks and a screech of tires told me different. Like a pack of dogs, they were after me.

Ragged breath tore out of my chest as I pumped my arms and legs harder than I ever had before. My board bumped against my stomach as I ran. I'd already thrown away the bag of food, but needed to hide my board so it wouldn't get stolen. I couldn't keep running with it. I heard shouts behind me. The pack was getting closer. Barely stopping, I tossed it into a bush beside a dumpster.

Racing down alleys and taking hard turns to throw them off, I saw the river up ahead. It was easier to run now without the board and I put more distance between me and them. My heart hammered in my chest. Crossing another major street before the light changed, I sailed down a side street that ended in the riverbank. It was a dead end. I paused to listen. Were they close?

The old train bridge rose above the river, rusted and unused. If I was fast, I could climb it before they found me. Grabbing on to the steel girders, I swung my legs up. Memories of the parking garage flooded through me as I pulled myself up to stand on the first supports. Powdery red dust coated my hands. Inside the guts of the bridge, it was dark and quiet, like a cave. Dragging myself up higher and higher, I moved with one focus, to get to the top.

Sweat ran into my eyes by the time I rolled onto the wooden decking. My arms ached and my fingers were blackened, bloody and throbbing. Peering over the edge, I looked for the kids. They'd branched off and only two of them jogged down the street searching for me. With an exhalation of relief, I flopped back down. Through cracks between the boards, I saw the river swirling and rushing under me. A stick floated by and then got sucked under by the current. I waited for it to reappear, but it didn't.

Crawling behind a girder, I stayed hidden from the street as my heart returned to a normal rhythm. From behind, the wind blew, uninterrupted and powerful, whipping my hat off, suspending it within an arm's length, taunting me and then letting it sail up and away. "Shit!" I said, panicked again. I watched as it floated down to the river. Two groups of kids had met up. My hat landed in the river near to them and from my hiding spot, I saw one kid point it out, his excitement obvious as he yanked on his friend's arm. They turned their heads, dispersing with renewed energy to find me.

One kid didn't move, but followed the path of where the hat had come from and looked up. Hidden by the girder, I squeezed my eyes shut and waited.

"He's up there!" I heard the shout, torn away by the wind, bring the others. My heart pounded, filling my chest with its vibration. I had to run, cross to the other side and lose myself in the streets of a neighborhood I didn't know. The muddy water swirled below me. What other choice did I have?

A voice was carried up to me on the wind. "Jump!" it said. Growing louder, the voices rose in a rhythmic beat. "Jump! Jump! Jump!" The kids below pounded on the girders, sending the vibration up through my feet.

My mind went blank. The voices grew louder, hungrier, threatening me. Gripping the steel beams, the rusty metal rough like sand paper, I leaned forward. My body bowed away from the bridge, high above the water. They'd never follow me into the river. I could float downstream and swim to shore. But, watching water froth in the current, I knew how violent the river could be. If I survived the impact, I might get sucked under. With a choked sob, I closed my eyes. The wind carried their words up to me, nudging me from behind, encouraging me to do it. Jump.

CORY

Cory woke to feet pounding through the house the next morning. He closed his eyes and pulled his blanket over his mouth to hide a gloating smile. His mom tried the doorknob, but he'd remembered to push the dresser in front of it. She hammered on the door. "Cory! Wake up! Open this door!"

Languidly, Cory got out of bed, moved the furniture and opened the door. A vein throbbed in the center of her forehead and stringy tendons stood out on her neck. "Someone vandalized my car!"

"Huh?" He rubbed his eyes.

"The windshield! They smashed my windshield!" Her voice rose to a piercing shrill. "What time did you get home?"

"It was like, two or something. Elmer's car was in the way. I moved your car so I could put Dad's in the garage." Cory stood in his boxers, his voice still thick with sleep.

"Yeah, I noticed that. And if you hadn't taken the corvette and moved my car, it wouldn't be smashed up!"

A hot flush spread to his face. "You're blaming me? Why's it my fault some kid smashed your window?" he growled at her.

She stepped back, suddenly aware that he towered over her. "You aren't supposed to take his car without my permission. But, as usual, you didn't listen." Her mouth twisted into a scornful pucker. "If my car had stayed in the garage, none of this would have happened. It's just a good thing they didn't go after Elmer's car!"

"Elmer's car? You're worried about Elmer's car? What if they'd smashed Dad's car? Would you even have cared? Or have you been too busy screwing Elmer to remember him?"

His mom's face crumbled. A soundless, ugly cry contorted her face and she reached back and hit him across the cheek with an open palm. Cory's cheek stung and he tasted warm, metallic blood in his mouth. Without thinking, he pushed her away, harder than he meant to, and she slammed her head against the wall. She stared at him like he was a stranger.

Cory glared at her across the hallway. The unspoken accusation of who had taken a baseball bat to her car hung between them.

Slamming his door shut, he pulled the dresser in front of it. Her footsteps receded in the hallway.

Soon after, he heard a tow truck's winch hauling the car away and his mom saying goodbye to Michelle. Cory realized that Elmer had been in the house the whole time. Cory tossed his lamp across the room. *What a cowardly bastard! He didn't even have the balls to stand up to me!* The front door shut and Cory closed his eyes. He couldn't stay here. He couldn't look at her anymore. And he couldn't deal with the resentment in her eyes: a constant reproach for his dad's death. Never once had she said it wasn't his fault. She'd never offered her forgiveness to him. Instead she'd moved on with her life while and let the accident hang over him, like a blade of a guillotine.

Michelle knocked on the door. "Cory?" She called to him. When he opened the door her eyes were red and puffy. Tracks from tears shone on her face. "What did you do? Mom and Elmer are going to the police station to file a report. Is it because of Mom's car?" She started to wail, "They're going to make you leave, Cory. I'll be all by myself!" She'd worked herself up into hysterics and the words were mangled by strings of saliva that flew out of her mouth as she cried.

Cory's nostrils flared as he thought. He'd given his mom a way to get him out of the house. She couldn't prove he'd done anything to the car, but he'd pushed her and he knew she could call it assault if she wanted to. Would it matter to the cops that she'd slapped him first?

"Shit!" He needed to think clearly. "Did you see Mom slap me this morning? Were you watching?"

She nodded her head.

"I peeked out my door when I heard you arguing." She took a deep breath and wiped the tears off her cheeks.

"Okay, good," Cory nodded. "If the police come, tell them that and call me. I'm going out for a while." Michelle's eyes grew wide.

"Are you coming back?" Clutching his arm, she dug her heels into the carpet. "You didn't do anything wrong."

He pushed her hands away. "It doesn't matter what I say. The cops won't believe me."

"Not if I tell them she's lying."

Cory turned to his sister in surprise. There was a familiar confidence in her eyes. He shook my head at her. "No, it's my problem. I'll deal with it."

Michelle raised her chin and wiped away the last remnants of tears. "I can't lose you too."

BEN

The rhythmic chanting stopped. For a minute, all I heard was the roar of the wind in my ears. Then, a deep male voice echoed. "Move away from the bridge. All of you!" I opened my eyes. A police cruiser, its light flashing, was parked below. An officer with a megaphone said something to his partner and pointed up at me.

A wave of nausea rolled over me. If I climbed down, I'd be safe while the cops were around, but what would happen when they left? Moving away from the edge, my head got hot and my hands started to sweat.

"You, on the top, climb down!" My hands shook too much to hold the girders. Below, the kids huddled together, separate from the cops. Lowering myself down, one foot touched a beam and my stomach scraped against the wooden decking. The kids were watching, waiting for me to get to the bottom, muttering amongst themselves. With a grunt, I dropped to the ground rubbing sweat and dirt off my hands. Dark smears stained my jeans.

The cop bellowed at us. "Clear off, all of you! Kids have drowned playing around the river." He must have thought we were all hanging out together; that I was one of them. Didn't he notice the hateful looks they shot my way? Or that I stood apart from them, unwelcome in their group? "Go on, get out of here," he ordered us. Taking off with a quick pace, I walked past the cruiser, the opposite direction of the other kids. "Hey, you," one of the cops called to me. I looked up, not breaking stride but slowed when I saw his face. He looked familiar and walked towards me. "Weren't you at the parking garage last week? The night your—" he broke off.

    I nodded. It was the younger cop from the night Luke fell.

    He gave me a long look. "Why'd you climb up there?"

    It was just the two of us. The kids, prodded by his partner, were crossing to the side street.

    I looked at my shoes, covered in brown dust and shrugged.

    He gave a resigned sigh when I didn't say anything. "Thought you'd be more careful seeing what happened last week."

    "Can I go?" I asked.

    "Yeah, but stay away from heights," he warned.

    As I walked off, he called to me again. "Your friends went that way."

    "They're not my friends," I muttered and kept walking.

Going home was like playing a game of capture the flag, except there wasn't anything fun about it. First, I had to get my board back, and staked out the alley where I'd hidden it, waiting by some garbage cans to see if anyone appeared. Creeping down the alley and ducking behind bushes every time a car drove by, I found it safe behind the dumpster and hugged it against me. Now, to get home.

    Worried that the kids knew where I lived—maybe one of them had even thrown the rock—I took a long route home, down alleys and quiet streets. I stayed out of sight as I got closer to my house, lurking around trees and in the back alley. The streetlights hummed as they flicked on. The air had grown colder

The Fall

and I shivered. My shirt, still damp with stale sweat clung to me. Peering out from behind a parked car, I could see my house. It was across the street, the cardboard flat and dark in place of a window. Fishing my keys out of my pocket, I ran my fingers over the familiar indentations. With one final scan of the street, I gripped the key in my hand and made a dash for my house, my heart beating in my head.

As I raced across the street, a car roared to life, its headlights blazing. Startled, I jumped a foot in the air, clutched my chest and yelped. Were they after me? Did I hear any footsteps closing in on me? Fumbling with the key, I tried to get it into the lock and look behind me at the same time. A girl in her twenties strolled from her house to the car, waving at the driver. I almost fell down with relief, laughing at myself. Shutting the door behind me, I put my board down and slid to the floor, shaking and crying.

I had a shower and tossed my clothes in the laundry, hoping Mom wouldn't ask why they were so dirty. Adrenaline raced through me and I couldn't sit still. Every time a car's headlights shone through the window, I ducked and peeked out. Three times, I checked to make sure no one had snuck in through the back. I kept the TV down low so I'd hear any unusual noises and held my cell in my hand so I could call 911.

As I calmed down, I started thinking about what would have happened if the cops hadn't shown up. I'd been ready to jump. It was a better option than getting swarmed by a mob of kids. They might have thrown me in the river anyway. Poetic justice for what they thought I'd done to Luke.

I closed my eyes. A dull ache throbbed in my head. They could find me again if they wanted. I couldn't hide in my house forever.

But I could move. My eyes flew open at the idea. I could go to live with Dad. It would mean a new school, new neighbourhood, new friends. It would also mean leaving Mom and Tessa. Mom would be mad. She'd probably offer to move to a different neighbourhood, rather than have me live at Dad's. But, I knew she couldn't afford a move, or to buy a new place.

But, Dad? The thought of suddenly being thrown together with him was laughable. I'd only been to his apartment once. Empty, except for a recliner, a TV and his unmade bed, it looked more like a motel room than a home.

What would Dad say if I asked? I imagined the heavy pause in our conversation as he tried to figure a way out, something reasonable to explain why I couldn't move in. Or, maybe he'd just say no and disappear.

Lost in thought, I forgot my phone was in my hand and jumped when it buzzed with a text from Ev. "Skatepark by the trax @ 4 on Tues. Last chance." My stomach clenched. It was after school, I could guarantee there'd be kids there. Did I want to risk my life for a sponsorship?

Last chance.

Between being chased by an angry mob, close to losing my shot at a sponsorship and Cory circling me like I was prey, I was a frayed rope, coming undone one string at a time.

CORY

The gun was heavier than he thought it would be, but warm, since Rico had just pulled it out of his jacket pocket. "Just in case," Rico had said as he handed it over.

Cory had never held a gun before and liked how comfortably it rested in his hand. "Nothing makes a guy feel like a man more than holding a gun. No one messes with you."

"You need to pick your spot," Rico instructed Cory as they cruised in Johnny's car. "We need cash, maybe something we can sell like electronics, cell phones, shit like that."

Johnny nodded from the front seat. "My first time, I hit a convenience store and scored some cigarettes, a bit of cash and lots of magazines," he winked at Cory. "I think those magazines all ended up in Rico's room, didn't they bro?"

"What'd you hit?" Cory asked Rico.

He turned from the front seat to look at Cory. "I made a restaurant. Nothing flashy, but they kept all their cash in the back. I used to work there when I was a kid. Made out with over a grand."

They passed discount stores, pool halls, churches and some medical clinics. Nothing felt right. He wanted his first robbery to mean something.

Turning down a back alley, he spotted a shaggy-haired blond kid lugging boxes to the garbage. *Ben.* Cory hadn't seen him since the night Luke fell. "Slow down," he said to Johnny. "I need to check something out."

Ben's eyes widened when he realized it was Cory. A thrill of excitement at the fear he'd inspired in the kid ran through him. A sign on the back door said *Plate-o's Greek Cuisine.* "Drive around the front again. I think I found the place." Through the front window, Cory could see the chairs stacked on the tables. An old man standing by the register clapped Ben on the shoulder.

Cory snickered as Johnny tore off. "That's the place, that Greek restaurant. I'll grab the cash in the register and look for a safe. There should be some booze too. And check out that flat screen."

Rico caught his eye in the rearview mirror. "Front or back?"

Cory thought. "Front. I'll break the window. No one hangs around this street at night."

"Okay. You wanna go back to Brewster?" Johnny lit a cigarette, took a puff and exhaled out the window.

"Yeah, sure." Cory knew time was going to pass slowly between now and when he hit the restaurant. Going back to his house wasn't an option. Michelle hadn't texted him. His mom had probably taken away her phone. Or maybe Michelle realized it was impossible to repair the damage that had been done.

Kira hadn't texted him either. She was probably still pissed off about the other night.

"That's it, bro. You're one step closer to being a Warrior."

Cory smirked to himself. He could have knocked off a different restaurant, but robbing the place Ben worked seemed more meaningful. Would the kid think it was a coincidence? Or would he realize that Cory had the power to make his life a nightmare.

BEN

Mom shook me awake. "Ben, wake up! We have to go to see Mama and Papa." I squinted at my alarm clock. It was four in the morning.

"Why, what happened?"

"Someone broke into the restaurant. Mama's so upset the police can't understand her. They need us."

With no traffic, we were at the restaurant in a few minutes. A cruiser had pulled up in front. The same two officers who had been at our house the night before were asking Mama and Papa questions. Papa's normally olive skin was pale. His thick, black hair stood on end like he'd been electrocuted. Mama was in her housecoat and slippers.

"Oh, dio, Patti! Ei-yi-yi, look what they do!" Mama Pal dragged Mom by the arm into the restaurant. Our feet crunched on glass from the broken window. A few of the chairs we'd recovered that afternoon had been thrown around and tables overturned. Framed pictures of Greek cities were either on the floor or hanging at odd angles. The self-serve pop cooler had been smashed and we had to step around puddles on the floor from the exploded cans. The cash register lay dented on the floor, as if someone had swung a baseball bat and knocked it around like a piñata; its cash drawer was open and empty. All the food in the industrial fridge had been dumped on the floor and the freezer door had been left open, which meant all Mama's sauces and meat were destroyed.

Papa closed his eyes at the sight of the usually pristine kitchen. It looked like a wrecking ball had hit it. Every dish had been broken, the white china lay in shards at our feet and all over the counter. The knives, pots and pans and utensils had been dumped on the floor.

Mom's lips pulled in thin and tight when she saw the mess. I felt like I'd been kicked in the stomach. The restaurant was their whole life, and it had been destroyed.

The cop with the mustache wandered over and wrinkled his brow. "Weren't we just at your house?" he asked. "Someone threw a rock?"

Mom stared at the disaster and nodded.

Frowning, the cop flipped through his notebook. He looked more closely at Mom and me, "What's the connection between you and the owners?" He asked.

"I used to work here. They're like family. Ben does work for them sometimes," she answered breathlessly, emotion close to the surface.

He turned to me. "Any idea who might have done this? Anyone you know who just joined a gang? Some of them use a B and E as an initiation. Although," he looked around and raised an eyebrow, "based on the damage, it could have been personal."

My mouth went dry. Cory. It couldn't have been a coincidence that I'd seen him that afternoon, sitting low in a car with gang members.

"Ben?" Mom's voice was sharp.

"What?"

As soon as she heard the crack in my voice, she gave me a hard look. "What is it?"

"Nothing." It felt like the noose around my neck was squeezing tighter, the rope burning into my neck so I couldn't breathe. I was getting backed into a corner. What did Cory want from me?

The officer raised his eyebrows at me.

"What happens now?" Mom asked, drawing his attention away from me. "Do we call the insurance company? Or wait for the police report?" She motioned for Mama and Papa to come over and explained what the officer said.

He took another look around, "Board up the windows and call your insurance company. We'll write up a report and let you know if anything develops."

Mama sniffled and rolled her eyes to the ceiling, as if calling on help from a higher power.

"It'll be okay, Mama. We'll get it all cleaned up good as new," Mom said. Her words sounded confident, but the deep line carved between her eyebrows showed her worry.

Papa caught my eye and made a sign of the cross at the picture of the Virgin Mary that hung over the sink. The safe hidden behind it had gone untouched. All their valuables were stored there, Mama's jewelry, their will, insurance papers. At most, the thief would have gotten $200 from the float in the register.

The Fall

I forced myself to watch Mama and Papa as they muttered in Greek and shuffled around the restaurant. I hadn't broken a window or swung a bat, but I felt responsible and hated that the people I loved were suffering because of me.

Monday

BEN

Sleep was impossible. Too many things ran through my head and no matter which way I turned in bed, nothing felt right. Finally, I gave up and went into the kitchen. Mom sat in the dark, slumped over the table. Still wearing her jacket, her purse lay in her lap.

Sitting down beside her, I rubbed my eyes. The corners of her mouth turned down in a frown. She looked lost in thought.

"Have you been here since we got home?" I asked.

She nodded her head. "I couldn't sleep."

"Me neither," I answered quietly.

She took a deep breath, audible in the silence. "Ben, you've got to tell me," she put her head in her hands, and closed her eyes. The stress of the last few days was wearing her down, I could see it. "What is going on?" When she looked up, tears slid down her cheeks. She looked defeated. Cory had made a victim out of her too.

My throat constricted and a hot rush of tears welled in my eyes.

I'd done this to her.

Telling her the truth about Cory and the kids chasing me would only scare her more. And there was nothing she could do. The kids had come after me, not because of what I'd done, but because of Cory's lies. I hated myself for not fighting back.

TAZ

The first time he'd walked onto the roof of the building and stared down at the sidewalk, his heart had started to pound. How could he sit on a wooden plank, lower himself to the ground and wash windows without thinking of Luke's body thudding to the ground?

Russ, already hooked onto anchors on the roof, had lowered himself down and was swinging off the side of the building. He'd called up to him. "You ready?" Taz had taken a deep breath. Wiping the sweat off his hands, he'd clipped the harness, grabbed on to the straps and pushed off. His feet had dangled in the air and his breath came fast. But, as he'd gained confidence in the security of the roof anchors and the strength in the ropes, he'd started to relax, enjoying the feeling of being weightless, like a little kid on a swing.

After that first day, Taz didn't worry about falling, instead, he took deep inhalation of air that hadn't been tinged with exhaust fumes, cigarette smoke or rotten garbage. He listened to the quiet, as street sounds died away. It was just him and Russ working together on the scaffold. Dip, rub, rub, streak, streak, wipe. Dip, rub, rub, streak, streak, wipe. There was a satisfying rhythm to window washing, leaving no space to think about his dad or their past. Instead, he thought about Luke. Memories of the night Luke fell had settled in him like a dull ache. He welcomed them. They weighed him down and if Russ ever saw his lips moving as he had a conversation with his brother, he didn't say anything.

After work, Taz intentionally drove up Kira's street hoping to meet her as she walked home from school. He'd been thinking about her. When he saw her turn down her street, he didn't scare her by honking, but called her name. She waved and smiled at him.

"Do you want a ride?" Taz asked tossing a fast-food restaurant bag filled with garbage and a couple of half-full water bottles into the backseat. He hadn't changed and could smell the ammonia of the washer fluid on his clothes.

She climbed in and they sat quietly for a while. The open windows brought in sounds from outside, kids laughing in the playgrounds, cars going by and some road crews jackhammering the streets.

"So, the funeral is tomorrow." Kira glanced at Taz from under her hair.

"Uh, it is?" The news had caught him off guard. No one had told him.

She nodded, but wrinkled her forehead in confusion. "That's what they said at school."

Taz snorted. "My dad kicked me out. He probably hopes I don't show." His mom could have called to tell him, but she hadn't. Had his dad turned her against him too?

Kira's eyes grew wide. "He was your brother!" She stared at him. "Luke would want you to be there."

Taz sniffed and turned to the window hoping the breeze would dry his eyes. The window-washing gig was screwing with his mind. Too much time to think.

"Why'd he kick you out?"

Shrugging, Taz swallowed.

"He probably blames you for Luke, right? Cuz you were there, but couldn't save him?" She spoke quietly.

"Yeah," Taz rubbed the nape of his neck. "My dad and I didn't get along too well before...." He let the sentence trail off.

"God." She leaned her head back against the headrest. "It's got to be hard for them. To lose their kid that way. And now he's pushing you away too." She turned to him, "I always thought you were kind of a jerk, you know. Kind of a loud mouth," she bit her lip and looked at him.

He gave her half-smile and she continued.

"You seem different now. Quieter, more..." She searched for the word. "Calm."

When Taz pulled up to her house, she unclicked her seat belt and turned to him. "Thanks for the ride," she said, but didn't make a move to get out of the truck. He was close enough to reach a hand behind her head and pull her to him. He wanted to kiss her. Their eyes locked and he knew she would have let him.

"See you tomorrow," he said and put the truck in drive.

Nodding, she pushed the door open and hopped out.

BEN

Dumping out my underwear drawer on my bed, I dug through to find the switchblade. One of the artifacts of Dad's presence I'd hung onto. It was the size of my hand, heavy, with a black case and a button that popped out a shining, metal blade. Snapping it back into place, I pulled the hood of my sweatshirt over my head and dropped the knife into my pocket. Let them come at me again. This time, I'd be ready.

I couldn't skate for the guys from Rox cold. I had to get out there and practice. Plus, my body craved Benjiland. Heading to a park downtown, in the middle of the day was still risky, but sitting home all day, jumping every time I heard voices outside was making me crazy. Some of my anger had left, replaced with wariness. But, no matter what, I wasn't going to be a victim of Cory's lies anymore.

As I put my board on the sidewalk and pushed off, the knife clunked against the back of my leg. When I got to the bus stop, my fingers brushed it as I dug out change for bus fare and it pressed into my leg when I grabbed a seat at the back of the bus. My neighbourhood rolled past me and I wished I could stay on the bus and just keep travelling, onto the highway and out of the city. Tall office buildings and people walking briskly in business suits with brief cases appeared. Downtown buzzed with activity. Hopefully, the skatepark, near the river on the other side of downtown, would be quiet. Slumping in the seat, my stop came up too soon.

The skatepark was almost empty. A few stoners sat on the edge and didn't even look at me when I put on my helmet and pads. The occasional whiff of pot smoke rolled my way and I raised my eyebrows at their boldness. My phone buzzed with a text. "At ur house. Where r u?" It was Tessa. I laughed with relief. Finally, after days of waiting, she wanted to see me.

"Sk8park downtown. U comin?"

"4 real?"

"y not?"

"What happened to ur window?"

I didn't answer. She knew where I was. If she really wanted to know, she'd come find me. Dropping my board into the bowl, I pushed off to the other side and back again, content to feel the

The Fall

vibration of the wheels on concrete. Landing a few tricks, and taking a massive bailout on one of them, I took a break. A kid across the bowl stared at me. He pulled out his phone and sent a text.

I stared at him. He looked up and then continued to text. Had he recognized me? Taking off for a lap with a powerful push, I ended up near him. He looked up, startled and put his phone away. He was younger than me with brown hair swept to the side. "Hey," I said, "What are you doing?"

The kid looked behind him. "Me?" he asked.

"Yeah, I saw you with your phone. Who were you texting?" I pulled myself up and stood beside him. He squinted up at me in the sun. About fourteen, he didn't look familiar, but I didn't know many of the younger kids who went to Tucker.

His eyebrows shot up. "Why?"

I knelt down to his level. "Did you send out a message that I was here?" He leaned back as I moved closer.

"No. Should I?"

His chippy attitude bothered me. What if he'd posted something online? Kids would show up looking to give me a beating. I needed to know who he'd texted. "Gimme your phone."

"Fuck off," he said with a sneer.

I felt for the knife. It was there if I needed it. "Don't be an asshole. I need to check your phone. I'll give it back." I used my most menacing tone.

He scrambled up. "Check it for what? You're a fucking lunatic." Scanning the park, the smirk disappeared. He looked worried.

"Just give me your phone," I said again. A note of desperation tinged my words. What if he ran away? I'd never know if I was in danger. Reaching into my pocket, I wrapped my fingers around the knife and pulled it out, the switchblade button under my thumb. "I'm not joking." I pressed the button. The blade clicked out, glinting in the sun.

"Holy shit!" he breathed when he saw it. He backed away and held up his hands. "Take my phone, take it!" His eyes grew wide with fear and the color drained out of his face. He pulled it out of his pocket and tossed it at me. It landed at my feet and the cover broke off.

"Daniel?" A woman's worried voice called out from somewhere in the park. "Daniel?"

Relief flooded his face, he'd been saved.

Saved from me. The realization that I was the one terrorizing him sent shock waves through my body. Grabbing my board, I tore off. What had happened to me? I was becoming one of them. Clicking the blade down, I dropped the knife into my pocket as I ran.

Veering off the main path, I took a smaller one that led to the river. It was quiet and tree-covered. I took some deep breaths to steady myself. The path followed the curve of the river and I slumped down on the ground, my back resting on a short wall and held my board up over my face, digging its tail into the gravel. Pressing my forehead against the rough grip tape, I felt hot, shame-filled tears prickle behind my eyes.

The knife rested heavily in my pocket. I pulled it out and, with a grunt, threw it into the river. The splash was unsatisfying, nothing more than a restrained plop. Would the police be looking for me? Carrying a concealed weapon, attempted robbery, uttering threats: they could probably get me on at least that many charges. What the hell had I been thinking?

Pulling my board closer to my body, I huddled behind it, wishing I could disappear. Wouldn't that be easy, to fall into the river, get sucked under, spinning and swirling, and never surface?

My phone buzzed with a text, the vibration jolting me back to reality. "I'm here. Whr r u?" It was Tessa.

"Just left." A guilty knot formed in my gut. I was pushing away the people who loved me. I didn't want them to know what I'd turned into. Yanking my sweatshirt over my head, I stuffed it in a garbage can. I couldn't risk bumping into Tessa on the bus. It was a long walk home and as soon as school was out, I would be a dead man if anyone saw me.

Things had spiraled so far out of my control since the night Luke died, I couldn't hold on to anything. Skating, Mom, Tessa, the restaurant; nothing that used to be normal was anymore.

Cory was behind all of it. I'd known it when he'd driven by me in the alley, staring at me with narrowed eyes and a malicious grin, hours before he'd hit the restaurant. He'd stolen my life from me. He hated me and there was nothing I could do to change it.

CORY

A fist caught Cory in the gut the second he walked into the clubhouse on Brewster. He clutched his middle and before he was upright, another punch hit him in the ribs. He went down to his knees. A kick to the kidneys and he thought he'd pass out. "Come on, Cory, you gotta do better than that," Johnny hauled him to his feet, the stink of booze heavy on his breath. A ring of twelve guys, mostly shirtless, stood around Cory. Their jeers and laughter weren't malicious, Cory's breathing slowed. He was getting beat-in.

He threw a few punches and caught one guy in the face, his knuckles swelled against the crack of bone. Suddenly, three guys were on him at once. Cory doubled over as they punched his face and back. His jaw ached and with the sickening crack of nose cartilage, a rush of warmth spread through his forehead. Johnny yelled at them to back off and Cory fell to the ground in a lifeless heap. The reprieve lasted for only a second before the beating continued. Cory fell in and out of consciousness as every time he tried to push himself to his feet, another fist or kick knocked him down. Leland's yell to stop registered in a fog of blood and pain. Willing himself to stand, Cory hauled his body upright and wobbled against Johnny, smearing his clothes with blood. One eye was already swollen shut, but he staggered in Leland's direction. "Got any beer?" Cory slurred, a trickle of bloody saliva hung from his mouth.

There was a roar of laughter from the rest of the Warrior Nation members and Cory collapsed onto a chair.

"You did good," Johnny said when he brought over a beer. It was ice cold and Cory downed most of it in one long gulp. "Most guys are out after two or three minutes, but you lasted almost four." He pointed to a chart on the wall behind Leland. Names and minutes were written in marker.

Cory snorted in agreement. "So that was the beat-in, huh?"

He nodded. "You're Warrior Nation now, bro." He clinked his beer against Cory's.

"What was yours like?" Cory asked Johnny. Two blurry images swayed in front of his eyes.

"I got blessed in, man. No beating, just the tat." He didn't say anything else, but Cory knew the circular scar on his chest hadn't come easy. Whatever he'd done to get it, the gang had been thankful for it.

Someone turned up the music and the house shook. Girls arrived and draped their arms around some of the older gang members. Cory ignored them and asked Johnny for another beer.

The Fall

Johnny signaled Dustin. He'd been leaning against the wall staring at Cory with a sour look on his face. "Go get Cory a beer," Johnny shouted over the music. Dustin hesitated, but turned towards the kitchen. "You still seeing Kira?" He examined his hand. Blood had started to congeal on his knuckles where he'd hit Cory.

"Yeah." Cory raised an eyebrow at Johnny and despite the pain, sat up straighter.

Johnny made a sound in his throat as if the news came as a surprise. "I saw her in your buddy Taz's truck."

The news didn't shock Cory. He knew Kira would find someone else, but he didn't think it would be Taz. The beat-in had dulled his senses. The anger that normally would have flared was suffocated.

He turned to Johnny. "Where?"

"Outside her house."

Cory dismissed it with a wave of his hand. "She thinks he's an ass. Luke was his brother. She's up—" his lips couldn't form the words properly. "Broken up over…" the thought trailed off.

Johnny slapped him on the back, sending a new wave of pain through his body. "You're one of us now. No one messes with a Warrior Nation's girl."

A chill ran through Cory. He didn't know if it was the beating, or the thought of Kira. She'd never take him back now, not as a gang member. One more person who was dead to him.

He snorted. "Hell with her. Stuck-up bitch." The words tasted wrong in his mouth, gritty with untruth.

Johnny shrugged, maybe disappointed that he couldn't help his new recruit.

Just before he blacked out, Cory marveled at how Johnny's scar gleamed in the dim light.

BEN

My heart bounced in my chest when I saw someone sitting on the front steps. Ducking behind a car, I peeked through a window to get a better look. Two braids, a skateboard and a black tuque: Tessa.

"I can see you, Ben," she called out.

Swearing under my breath, I emerged from my hiding place. She was going to grill me with questions.

I walked up the steps and unlocked the door without talking to her. She followed me into the house. Once the door shut, she grabbed my arm and forced me to look at her.

"What the hell, Ben! What the fuck is going on with you?"

"What do you mean?"

She narrowed her eyes, the black eyeliner turning them into slits. "Were you wearing your red sweatshirt today?"

My cheeks flushed. "No."

She rolled her eyes. "You are such a shitty liar. Cops at the skatepark asked if I'd seen a blond kid wearing a red hoodie. He tried to mug somebody." She stared at me incredulously. "It was you, wasn't it?"

The blush deepened and I clenched my teeth, the muscles in my jaw taut and ready to snap. "What's going on with you?" She asked again.

I squeezed my hands into fists. "Why is everyone asking me that?" Maybe if I went on the offensive, she'd leave me alone.

"Why do you think? I heard about the kids coming after you. They were bragging about it. Your locker's covered with graffiti and when I rode up, some guys had just finished replacing your window." She glowered at me, her cheeks flushed. "So, yeah, I'm a little curious." She stood back, her arms crossed over her chest.

I tried to bite back my emotions, but they were too close to the surface. The first words came out raspy, my voice strangled. "Everyone hates me. The window … that was a few nights ago. When they chased me, I got to the top of the old train bridge," the next part was hard. I willed myself to keep going and closed my eyes so I wouldn't chicken out. "I think I would have jumped. Just to get away from them. And then, Cory, I think he broke into Mama and Papa's restaurant," I took a wavering breath, "because of me. He destroyed the place."

Tessa's eyes got big and she stared at me. "Shit, Ben," she whispered.

"And today, I needed to skate, like I can't handle this anymore, Tessa. I just needed to get on my board, but I knew, that if the kids showed up again … I brought the knife, but I didn't think I'd use it. Then, I saw that kid on his phone, and I snapped."

Some of the anger returned. It was Cory's fault I'd been pushed into a corner like this. Pulling a knife on a kid? That was an act of desperation.

"Oh my God. Why didn't you tell me?"

"What would you have done? Been my bodyguard? Anyway, you were mad at me."

Tessa closed her eyes, wincing. "I'm not that big of an asshole, am I?"

"Sometimes," I said, and shirked away from the swat she gave me.

"What about the funeral. Are you still going? All those kids will be there. And Cory."

"You were the one who said I should tell Cory off, remember?"

She flinched, "That was before I knew how bad it was."

"I'm meeting the guys from Rox after the funeral. At the skatepark."

Tessa raised her eyebrows. "So, even if you don't go to the funeral, they could still get you at the skatepark."

"Way to think positive," I snorted.

She fiddled with the zipper on her sweatshirt, buzzing it up and down. "It's fake to go to someone's funeral that I never knew, but I'll go if you want me to."

"Really?"

She nodded. "See. I'm not such an asshole." She picked up her board. "I better go. I'll meet you outside the church tomorrow, okay? Try not to get beat up before I get there."

Watching Tessa leave, I realized what a difference it would make having her by my side. I knew I had to face Cory, but I couldn't do it alone.

Tuesday

TAZ

The house didn't look any different, somehow that surprised Taz. A rusty lawn chair with a faded seat cushion still sat on the front porch beside a chipped clay pot with last summer's flowers. The doorbell chimed and he heard his mom shuffle to the living room window to see who it was.

She opened the front door, but kept the screen between them. He'd never seen that black dress before. She must have bought it for the funeral. And she'd put on makeup. Her slippers were the same. The fur had been rubbed off in patches so only the mesh fabric showed through; they looked like a dog's coat with ringworm. He closed his eyes against the image of the swollen, purplish flesh around her ankles.

She took a sharp intake of breath and leaned against the screen. "Taz. What are you doing here?"

"So, today's the day, huh? Why didn't you tell me?" He tried to keep the accusing tone out of his voice. He wanted to give her a chance to explain.

She looked away. "He didn't want me to." Closing her eyes and shaking her head, he watched as flashes of emotion crossed her face. "I should have called. It's just so hard." Her voice cracked and she started to cry. Wiping her eyes, she cleared her throat. "He's going to be home any minute. You should go before he sees you."

Now she was sending him away too. Taz set his mouth in a grim line and turned to go. What the hell had he been thinking?

"Wait." The door opened and she reached out to grab his arm. Her eyes, Luke's eyes, were remorseful. She let the screen door slap shut behind her. Taz looked at her, not as a son, but as a stranger. What would anyone walking down the street think about this overweight woman with bags under her eyes and a mouth puckered from too many cigarettes.

"It's quiet around here," she said watching the street. "Half the time the only noise is when I wash the dishes. I tried to clean out his room yesterday. Thought it might help." Her voice cracked and she buried her forehead in her hand. The flap of skin under her arms shook as she sobbed. "I found some things I thought you might like—" She tried to continue, but the words kept getting stuck in her throat "I put them in the garage."

Taz nodded. What would he do with them? He didn't have a place to live.

Her fingers itched for a cigarette, the yellowed nails flicked and twisted around each other looking for something to hold. Taz reached out and grabbed them. They felt reassuringly fleshy and warm. He couldn't remember the last time he'd held her hand.

The van pulled up to the curb. Taz felt his body stiffen.

"What the hell is he doing here?" Dennis slammed the car door shut and marched across the lawn.

Taz and his mom stood up. His dad's eyes blazed like hot coals. His hair lay matted in clumps around his head. Rage and beer had left his skin red and blotchy.

She looked at Taz helplessly. "Just go."

Taz stumbled off the front step onto the grass. *It doesn't need to be like this. Luke wouldn't like it.* The thought reverberated in his head. He wanted to pummel his dad, if that's what it took, to make him see that he was hurting too.

"Why'd you come here, anyway?" Dennis shouted from the porch.

Words stuck in his throat. He could never explain what had prompted him to come back, not in a way Dennis would understand. The wall between them was too tall, too thick with anger. Instead, Taz ignored him and walked to his truck. He got in and sat shaking in the seat.

Booze. Every fiber in his body called out for it, trembled for it. How else would he get through this day? He watched as his dad slammed the front door behind him, making the window glass rattle. His cell rang. It was Kira. He answered, but couldn't find the words to say hello.

"Taz, are you there?"

"Yeah." *I'm here.*

Her voice was shaky. "Can I come to the church with you? I mean, if you aren't going with your parents."

He put the truck in drive and barreled toward her house.

CORY

Cory woke up the next morning sore all over. It felt like someone had rearranged his insides into all the wrong spots and nothing fit in their new home. A whimper escaped his lips when he tried to sit up on the floral couch that smelled like cat pee. Dried blood had caked around his swollen lips and made it hard to open his mouth. A headache ripped his skull apart, but that was probably more from the beer and shots than the beating. He'd dreamed about his dad last night. They'd been in the car, after the accident, his dad was slumped over the steering wheel with a shard of glass sticking out of his jugular. Blood gushed like a fountain from his neck, but he didn't realize he was hurt. His eyes were bright and alert as he asked Cory how the 'vette was running.

Staggering to the door, he barely made it outside before he puked. His shirt smelled rank and splotches of blood stained his jeans. He needed to get some clean clothes before the funeral.

Michelle's eyes grew big when she saw Cory, as if her brother were a stray dog who'd wandered in. "Did you get mugged?" she said staring at the swollen, purplish bruises and cuts on his face. The one over the bridge of his nose still throbbed.

"It looks worse than it is." Pushing past her, he looked around. "Where's Mom?"

"She's shopping. Who did that to you?"

Cory thought she might cry. "Don't worry about me, okay, Mish? I'm fine."

She nodded, but looked unconvinced.

"Dad would have hated this," she blurted out. "We aren't a family anymore." Her lip trembled and tears started to fall as fast as she could wipe them away.

Turning away from her, his eyes landed on a family photo. It was framed on the mantle. They'd been at a friend's house on Canada Day. Seated at a picnic table, his dad had a beer in his hand and the other arm around his mom. Cory and Michelle sat across from them eating hot dogs, unaware anyone was taking a picture. It had been a good day. They'd come home late, smelling like smoke from the bonfire, the sound of popping firecrackers still in their ears.

A lump settled in Cory's throat. He didn't trust himself to speak. That picture felt like a lifetime ago.

"Can't you just say sorry to Mom and make it better? Stop hating her?"

He looked at the photo again. His mom was leaning on his dad's shoulder, a dreamy look on her face. He turned to her. "I don't hate her." *I just want her to love me again.* Cory wiped his eyes, surprised at the wetness smeared on his sleeve. "When she came to get me at the hospital after Luke fell, she looked at me, like 'This again?' He choked the words out. It's like she expected me to screw up and kill somebody else."

Michelle's eyes flared. "You didn't kill him!"

He pushed his fists into his eyes to stop the tears. "I was right there! I saw Dad die. And then I saw Luke. I was right there!" A sob broke through and Cory collapsed against a chair. "It could have been me, Michelle. Both times! Why wasn't it me?"

"I don't know, but it wasn't your fault." Michelle sank to her knees at his feet. "You and Taz and Luke were always doing stupid stuff. No one was surprised when it happened."

Her voice, or maybe her words, calmed Cory. Had the beatin messed with his head? He'd never allowed himself to talk like this before. It wasn't right. He needed to keep it all inside, where he could control it. "I hate myself," he mumbled.

Cory's mom cleared her throat. They hadn't heard her come in. She stood watching them from the kitchen.

There was a long moment of silence, everyone frozen in place like a staged portrait. "What happened to you?" she asked.

"Don't worry about it." Cory muttered. But, she dropped her shopping bags and knelt beside him, moving so close, he could smell her perfume.

"Did you go to the hospital? Some of those cuts look bad."

Cory pushed her hand away. "I said, don't worry about it."

She pinched her mouth and drew a deep breath. "You're my son, of course I worry."

Michelle threw him a pointed look. Don't freak out, her face said. Cory exhaled and met his mom's gaze. "I got jumped. I'm okay."

"Did you go to the police?"

He shook his head. "I don't think they'd be real concerned about it."

"Probably not," she said with an acerbic tone. "They didn't do much about my car, either."

He gritted his teeth against a retort and looked away.

"Where have you been staying, anyway?" The forced casualness of her tone belied her worry. Cory noticed the dark circles under her eyes and hoped that wondering where he was had kept her up at night. Michelle leaned in, curious.

"At a friend's."

"Anyone I—"

"No," he interrupted.

"Taz's?"

"No." Cory wanted the conversation to be over. "I just came by to pick up some things."

"You could stay for dinner. Elmer's coming over and we were going to barbe—"

He cut her off with a derisive laugh. "I'd rather eat shit and live in a sewer than have dinner with him."

His mom's face turned cold. "It looks like that's exactly where you've been living."

"Yeah, well, anywhere's better than here," he muttered loud enough for her to hear.

She puckered her lips like she'd tasted something sour and stood up. "I was trying, Cory. You just have to make everything so hard. What are you punishing me for?"

Michelle's eyes grew round and fearful.

Cory clenched his fists and stared at her. "For being alive."

His mom gasped. She turned and ran from the room, gripping the doorway on her way out to steady herself.

"You didn't have to say that!" Michelle railed at him.

"It's better if I'm gone, Mish. I can't be here, not with Mom around and Elmer"—he said the name like it was a communicable disease—"coming for dinner. If you need me, call me." Cory went to his room, stuffed some clothes in an old hockey bag that smelled like wet leather and tossed it in the backseat of the corvette. The funeral was in an hour and he had to pull himself together before then.

BEN

My stomach growled as I lurched down the hall to the kitchen. Mom was in her uniform with her hair pulled up into a ponytail for work. She stirred eggs in a pan with quick, choppy movements. She must be running late.

"Grab the juice," she said without looking up.

It sloshed in the carton. Barely half a glass left. I looked in the fridge for more, but besides some sour cream and pizza from a few nights ago, the wire shelves sat empty.

"I'll go shopping after work tonight," Mom sighed and dumped the yellowy eggs on two plates. She looked at the clock. "I have to leave in five minutes, but I want to talk to you."

Still rubbing sleep from my eyes, talking was the last thing I wanted to do. I needed to wipe the fuzz of my teeth first. I took a swig of the juice straight from the carton. Mom threw me a look, but didn't say anything.

"If it's about the funeral, Tessa said she'd go with me."

Mom looked up from her plate and nodded. "Good. I didn't want you to be alone. What about your dad? Did he say anything about it?"

"Yeah, he said he'd meet me there. But, you know...." No need to explain Jim's less than stellar record to Mom. "You got the money for the window, right? I left it in your room."

"I got it."

Draining the juice, I picked up my fork and pushed the lumpy eggs around the plate for a moment. "It's good he brought it over."

She took a breath and said "Yep" through tight lips. She swallowed a bite of eggs and fixed me with an intense look. "There's something else." Biting her lip, she lowered her voice. "I don't want you going to the skatepark anymore. Even with Tessa. It's too dangerous."

"Why?"

She scoffed. "Why? We had a rock go through our window and Mama and Papa's restaurant was broken into. Am I the only one who thinks it's a coincidence? This neighborhood is getting worse, not better," she muttered.

"No one's going to try anything out in the open," I lied. Of course, they would. "At least, not with Dad and Tessa with me."

She dropped her fork and stared at me. "So this *is* personal?"

I couldn't look at her.

"Is it because of Luke? What happened that night that you're not telling me?" Her voice rose and she leaned across the table.

The Fall

A blush spread up from my neck. I was caught. "It was after," I mumbled. "Cory started spreading lies about me. Saying I was the reason Luke fell."

Her forehead wrinkled in confusion. "Why would he do that?"

I shrugged, careful not to give too much away. "Looking for someone to blame, I guess." My heart started to beat faster. I was a shitty liar.

She eyed me carefully. "Has he come after you?"

I swallowed and let my hair flop over my eyes, forcing a laugh. "He's just being an asshole. It's not a big deal, Mom."

"I hope you're telling me the truth. There's no shame in asking for help, especially after the window. And the restaurant." The last words were loaded with meaning, but I didn't bite.

"Stuff like this happens all the time. Everyone will forget about it after the funeral." She eyed me suspiciously. It was hard to tell if she was buying my lies.

"Well, I still don't think you should go to the skatepark." She dropped her fork on her plate and carried it to the counter. "It won't kill you to wait a couple of weeks until things blow over."

I stayed silent. It didn't matter what she said. I'd already decided that I was going. Cory had taken enough from me, I wouldn't let him take my sponsorship too.

It was one of those perfect spring days. Warm sun, blue sky, light breeze; a perfect day for a funeral. Tucked behind the staircase of the old, stone church, I watched as Luke's friends, parents and teachers arrived. My stomach was in knots, worrying that someone would notice me.

Tessa sauntered slowly down the center of the sidewalk, forcing people coming in the other direction to walk around her. She had on a skirt, black tights and her clunky skate shoes. She had legs like a stork: skinny with knobby knees. She stared straight ahead and wore an angry scowl that turned into a smirk when she saw me.

"Nice pants," she said. The black pants Mom had bought me looked goofy with my skate shoes.

"Nice dress."

"Shut up. It's a skirt."

It was almost two o'clock. Scanning the sidewalk for signs of Dad, we started to walk up the stairs. I felt like an idiot for believing that he'd come through this time. "Ben!" I heard my name and turned to see Dad, slipping a tie over his neck as he ran, coming towards us. "Couldn't find a parking spot," he explained. Tessa threw me a look.

"Dad, this is Tessa."

His face broke into a smile. "Great to meet you."

Tessa gave him a once over and nodded in reply. I shot her a warning a look. Today was not the day to make a point about his parenting skills.

We squeezed into a pew at the back. Tessa, me and then Dad. It was packed. People stood shoulder to shoulder, whispering to each other. What would they do if they saw me? Craning my neck, I scanned the crowd for Cory's head, but couldn't find him. Was he sitting at the front with Luke's family?

Melting wax and a slight aroma of incense filled the damp air. It seemed like a weird place to hold a funeral for a guy like Luke. He'd probably never come here when he was alive, why would he want to be remembered here when he was dead?

An organ started to play. The doors opened and a priest in a white robe walked in ahead of Luke's parents. They walked together, but apart. Tears ran down his mom's cheeks and her lip quivered as she walked towards the casket at the front. Luke's dad stumbled down the aisle, as if an invisible rope was pulling him. Taz followed, a few paces behind his parents and all alone. He kept his eyes straight ahead. His body seemed disjointed with none of its usual fluid movement.

People who knew Luke got up to speak. Some barely made it through their speeches, overcome with emotion. Watching them, Dad sniffed and cleared his throat a few times, clapping a reassuring hand on my knee. "Must have been a good kid," he murmured. I didn't argue and kind of liked that Luke would be remembered that way.

We stood for a hymn, his friends and family rising as one. From the front of the church, Luke's mom started to sob, her cries echoing off the stone walls.

It could have been any of us lying in a coffin. It could have been my mom crying. The events of the night flashed through my head again. His body flailing in the darkness, the thud when he hit the ground and his last exhalation, choked with blood. I closed my eyes, my knees weak. He was *gone*. Dead. Just like that. In a second.

It was too much.

I thought I'd buckle, collapse, like a crumbling wall at my dad's feet. I felt Dad grip my shoulder, steadying me. His rough finger tips, dry like sandpaper, crackled against my shirt. His touch released the hot tears burning my eyes. Tessa looked at me, her dark eyes soft. She slipped her hand into mine and squeezed.

I was going under, drowning in my failure to stand up for myself. Cory, kids at school, they wanted to see me in pain, and I was letting them succeed, letting them take my grief and twist it against me.

I wouldn't go down, not the way Cory and those other kids wanted. They thought I was weak, a coward who ran, and they were right.

Steeling myself with a breath, I held Tessa's hand tighter. Luke's death had been senseless, a clumsy accident. But I was done letting his death and Cory's lies define me as a victim. It was time to fight.

I squinted against the bright sun. I'd kept my head down as people had filed past at the end of the service. After the somberness of it, no one had paid attention to me, but what would happen now that we were outside, surrounded by his friends and family? Without the dim church light to conceal me?

Taz stood close to the curb, shaking hands with some teachers from Tucker. He didn't look like the guy who'd dared his brother to race the train or the guy who'd been kicked out of a movie theatre. He looked serious. The loudmouth asshole had disappeared.

I wished I could say something to him, but what? "Sorry" didn't seem enough. Even after sharing the scariest, worst, most memorable night of our lives we were strangers. Had he fallen under the spell of Cory's lies? Did he want me dead like the rest of the school?

He scanned the crowd and his gaze fell on me. My mouth went dry, but I didn't look away. I wanted him to know I was here; that I was grieving for Luke too. Taz's brows furrowed and I held my breath, wondering if he'd shout out my name, drawing attention to my presence. Tessa stood stiffly at my side, one hand gripping my shirt sleeve, willing me to walk away. I stood my ground and stared back at him, sympathy plain on my face.

He held my eyes a moment longer and then nodded, bowing his head. Tears flooded my eyes, blurring the faces in front of me.

Dad, Tessa and I moved with the flow of people down the steps. No one noticed me. Their watery eyes were focused on Taz and his family. The car was parked a few blocks away and I let out a sigh of relief when we reached it, grateful that we didn't have to go to the burial. Dad had offered Tessa a ride home and I pulled the seat forward so she could squeeze into the backseat. "Still going to the skatepark?" she asked quietly while Dad walked around to the driver seat.

I set my mouth in a grim line, my resolve to fight still fresh in my mind. "Yeah. I'm done running from them."

She shot me a surprised look and grabbed my sleeve, forcing me to bend down beside her. She narrowed her eyes, searching my face. "Are you serious?"

I nodded and she grinned at me. "About friggin' time."

Dad settled into his seat. "What are you two whispering about?" he said with an overly friendly grin.

Tessa smirked at me. "Skateboarding. Hey," she said, as if the idea had just occurred to her, "You should watch Ben skate today. He's awesome. Some guys from a store are coming to see if they want to sponsor him." Tessa sat back and crossed her arms looking pleased with herself.

Dad turned to me. "That true, Ben? You're that good?"

I cleared my throat. I *was* that good. "Yeah, I am."

"Patti doesn't want Ben to go though."

"You're full of information today, aren't you Tessa?" I muttered.

Dad started the car and it sputtered to life. "Why doesn't your mom want you to go?"

"She thinks skating is a waste of time." It was partially true.

Dad flashed me a grin, as if he was my co-conspirator. "You're young. Now's the time to have some fun." He put the car in drive. "I guess you want to go home first to change?" he asked as he pulled into traffic.

"He's got a pair of jeans in his backpack," Tessa told him and sat back looking smug.

TAZ

Taz could feel people looking at him, the pressure of their eyes beat against his skull. He'd already shaken hands with the principal, an irony neither of them had acknowledged. How many times had Taz sat in his office, shooting hateful looks as he'd received a punishment? Now, they commiserated together as if they were relatives. Coach had come too, offering condolences to his parents and then embracing Taz. He'd almost lost it when Coach had grabbed his shoulder and given him a final, meaningful squeeze.

A black 'vette pulled up outside the church, behind the town car waiting to take Taz and his parents to the graveside burial.

His mom had asked him to join them, a whispered plea as his dad stared at the casket. "It's what Luke would have wanted," she'd said. Taz couldn't say no. He didn't want to. Luke was his brother as much as he was his dad's son.

Taz squinted, unconvinced that the guy stepping out of the sports car was Cory. His face was torn up, a kaleidoscope of bruises. Had he been jumped? He'd never seen Cory look so rough.

He walked down the steps towards his friend. Cory's cologne stung Taz's nostrils, heady and overpowering. They locked eyes, and Taz waited for a glimmer of the Cory he knew to appear. Why hadn't Cory been at the funeral, standing in the pew beside him? Taz suppressed the ball of anger that rolled up from his gut. He let his breath come and go with deep exhalations.

"Where were you?" The desperation in Taz's voice surprised him.

Cory recoiled, stepping closer to the car. He cleared his throat, shifting his eyes from Taz.

Taz got in his line of sight, "You should have been in there, man. He was like family to you!"

Cory's eyes flashed. "What the hell do you know about family?" he yelled. "You think I haven't thought about him everyday since he fell?" They stood toe-to-toe. If one made a move, the other was ready, every muscle taut.

Letting his shoulders fall, Taz felt the anger dissolve. He didn't have the energy to fight. "I needed you today, man," he said quietly.

Cory closed his eyes, and when he opened them, the hostility was gone. "Look at me, Taz. I'm a fucking mess."

"What happened?"

Cory hesitated, then leaned in. "I'm hanging with the Warriors now."

Taz narrowed his eyes at Cory. "They did this to you?" Cory's lip had split open as they were speaking and a thin coat of pinkish blood veiled his teeth.

"I got beat-in." He winced. "It was brutal." He straightened up, displaying his battered face with twisted pride. "I gotta look out for myself now, y'know?" He cocked his head at Taz, appraising him. "I can put a word in for you. Let them know you're interested."

"Taz!" His dad called. He was helping the priest climb into the front seat of the town car, tucking the man's white robe into the car. "Let's go," he said, slamming the door. He limped with exhaustion as he walked to the rear door.

Cory's eyes gripped his. "What d'you think? Be like old times. Me and you together." He raised an eyebrow, daring him to say no. Taz glanced at Dennis, now waiting for him, one hand on the roof of the black town car, the buttonholes on his white dress shirt gaped as the fabric stretched across his belly.

Taz shook his head and stepped back, sinking into the soft earth. "I can't think about shit like that right now."

Cory's face was unreadable.

"You're coming to the burial, right man?"

Cory stared at him. "I don't know."

Taz sniffed back emotion and turned away from Cory. They'd been best friends for years, done everything together, even watched Luke die together. "Forget it. Go hang with your new brothers."

As he walked away, Taz realized Cory hadn't said "I'm sorry." Complete strangers had said it, but not Cory. It bugged him that Cory held those two words back from him, as if his pain and loss didn't count. A lump formed in his throat, but it wasn't tears for Luke, it was anger at Cory.

Kira, huddled off to the side with a group of girls, was hidden behind the stone steps. She hadn't gone to Cory when he'd shown up. Were they over, now that Cory was a Warrior? Ducking into the car, he cast a glance at Kira. Her face, puffy and tear-stained, still looked beautiful. "I'm sorry," she mouthed. He closed his eyes and let her silent offering roll over him.

BEN

When we got to the skatepark, I grabbed Tessa's elbow. "I'm bringing it," I said, a slow smile of excitement tilted the corners of my mouth up. I hadn't been this pumped to skate since-I stopped the thought before it took root in my head. I needed to focus, forget about the last week, and get into a zone: to Benjiland.

Tessa nodded and held up her fist for a bump. "Do it."

We walked to a wooden picnic table gouged with graffiti. Shattered beer bottles crunched under our feet. Dad sat down and looked around him with a frown. We'd stopped at a gas station so I could change and Dad could get a coffee. He slurped it through the plastic lid, droplets glistened on his lips. "Good luck," he said as I strapped on my helmet and pads and grabbed my board.

Wind ruffled the fringes of hair not covered by the helmet. Grit under the wheels crackled and I picked up speed coming to the first small hill in the bowl. An easy jump. I did a Caspar flip when I got air and landed fakie. I pushed off again and went around a few times until I had enough speed to hit the half-pipe. With a burst of energy, I went over the edge, grabbed my board and spun once in mid-air coming down hard. Coasting over to the side near Dad and Tessa, I looked up. Dad clapped his hands over his head like he was at a rock concert. Tessa had sneaked away to the other side of the bowl and gave me a nod of encouragement.

I kick-flipped back into the transition and took another rip around the bowl. My breath and the motion of the board were like one movement. I did a long frontslide boardslide and ended with a 180. Every sensation was heightened: the sun on my skin, the vibration of my wheels, the fluffy dandelion fur that floated around me, the hollers from Dad.

When I stopped to take a break, Ev's legs were dangling in the bowl in front of me. Mitch was pacing behind him on his cell. "Hey, dude," Ev reached a hand down to clasp mine in greeting. "Looking good. Show me something else."

It was all the encouragement I needed. I pulled out all the stops, did every trick I'd ever tried and nailed them all. It was like I'd been dipped in honey, riding smooth and liquid around the bowl and sticking everything. By the time I glided around the coping to where they were sitting, Mitch was staring at me open-mouthed, his phone forgotten in his hand.

"Stellar," was all he said to me.

I sat down on the pavement beside Ev, breathing hard and smiling. Dad was still at the picnic table watching, but Tessa's eyes had travelled across the bowl to the parking lot. I didn't want to look. My whole life was riding on this one conversation.

"We're interested," Ev started, "but, you need to be committed. I mean, you gotta be skating every day, outside, inside and going to different skateparks. You gotta learn from the older guys too. Show us you can add to your style."

Mitch nodded. He was tall and skinny and with a shaved head, he looked like a tanned q-tip. "Come hang at the shop. You'll meet some real old school dudes. They'll love talking to you."

Ev nodded at Mitch. "Here's what we're thinking. There's an invitation-only competition at SK*t next weekend. We're gonna sponsor you and see how you do. We'll talk after that about gear."

"Okay," I said with a face splitting smile. "That's awesome."

"I'll text you the details tomorrow. Later." Ev offered his hand for a fist bump and Mitch waved as they walked to the parking lot.

I rolled my head back and felt the sun beat down on my face.

"What did they say?" Tessa asked, racing to the edge when they'd gone. Her eyes were shining with a smile, even though it barely registered on her mouth.

"I'm competing for them this weekend." I laughed. The thrill of saying it out loud ran through me.

"What about gear?"

"They're gonna wait to see how I do," I said walking away from the bowl and towards Dad.

She shook her head. "Man! You're gonna get a new deck, wheels, trucks, everything!" She played at jealousy, but I knew she was as excited about it as I was. "That last trick you did was wicked. I've never seen you do it before."

Dad had lit a cigarette and stubbed it out under his shoe when I got to the picnic table. Its smell clung to him and I backed away a bit. "I guess it was good news?" he asked.

"Yeah, they wanna sponsor me and I have a competition this weekend," I explained as I took off my helmet and pads and stuffed them into my backpack.

Dad slapped me on the back. "I guess it's a good thing you didn't listen to your mom, eh?"

My back stiffened. Who was he to make a comment against Mom? But, I let it go, not wanting to ruin the moment.

"Why don't we go grab a burger, you know, to celebrate?" Dad asked. He looked from me to Tessa, practically rubbing his hands together in eagerness. I wondered if hanging out with us made him feel like a dad, or just young again.

I was so buzzed from my skating, I didn't realize Dad was driving to a regular Tucker High hang-out. There were lots of kids, but instead of people laughing and goofing off, everyone sat huddled together in small groups, some still in their clothes from the funeral.

My stomach lurched at the sight of them. But, I set my mouth in a determined line. I wasn't going to keep running.

"Hey, Jim," Tessa piped up from the back. "Can we go somewhere else?"

"Why? We're already here." He unbuckled his seat belt and opened the door.

Tessa started to stutter an explanation, but I caught her eye and shook my head. "As soon as they see you, they're going to come after you!" she whispered. "Tell him you're scared so we can get out of here."

"No," I said through clenched teeth.

She gave an angry sigh and slumped back. "This is stupid. You're going to get your ass kicked in front of your dad." He stood waiting for us, cupping his hand around the flame of his newly lit cigarette and taking a puff.

"I have to deal with them," I told her.

This was it. If I didn't get out now and face these kids, what was the point of getting sponsored? How could I practice and go to competitions if I was always worried about who I'd run into?

"Come on, let's go." Grabbing my board, we walked to the restaurant.

We'd almost made it to the entrance when a group of guys walked out of the restaurant towards us. I thought they'd veer out of the way as we got closer, but when Tessa and I moved in one direction, so did they. We did that dance a few times until one of them barged right into me. I stumbled and collided with Tessa. She fell to the ground. A flash of white skin showed through a tear in the knee of her black stockings.

They started laughing at me and my face grew hot, surprise, fear and anger boiling together. Someone came from behind and ripped my board out of my hands. My fingers stung from the friction and one knuckle got caught on the axel. Blood welled and dripped down my hand. Spinning around, I saw Cory holding my board against a lamppost. When he had my full attention, he lifted it behind his shoulder and slammed it against the pole. Fragments of the deck sprayed in the air and half of it flew across the parking lot.

He threw the piece of skateboard still in his hands at my feet. I watched it skid across the parking lot, the griptape scraping against the pavement, and didn't see the first punch coming. It hit me in the gut and I doubled over, stumbling. The next one came from the left and sent me reeling past Tessa. Bile rose in my throat and I spit it on the ground. "You fucking pussy! It was your fault! It was your idea to climb!" His voice loud and harsh in my ears. I squeezed my eyes shut, waiting for the next one, but it didn't come.

I tried to stand and wobbled. He took another swing at me, but I dodged it. Cory stood breathing heavily, holding his side as if it hurt. A crowd surrounded us, but instead of the usual cheering and rabid excitement, they stood quiet, wary.

Tessa scrambled up to her feet and stood beside me. Her fingers curled like claws.

I raised my chin and looked Cory in the eye. A purple bruise circled it, the edges tinged green.

With a cough, I stood upright, my stomach tender and sore. "You're a liar." I exhaled. He came at me again, but with less focus. His punch fell short, and I easily avoided it. "You're a liar!" Crying and shouting at the same time, spittle flew from my mouth. "Climbing was your idea. No one would have followed *me* up there. Luke followed you." My voice, raw, echoed in the parking lot. I moved a step closer, coughing as I tried to take a breath. "Why weren't you at the funeral, Cory?" Kids around us started to whisper.

Cory seethed, baring his teeth as if he wanted to rip flesh from my bones.

I didn't back down. "After all this, it's you who's the coward."

He lunged at me, a guttural roar exploding from his throat. He knocked me down and got in a body shot, straight to the kidneys. I choked and gasped for air as pain shot up my spine. A second later, his weight was gone. Opening my eyes, I saw him struggling against three other guys who'd grabbed him by the arms. They pulled him away as he spit and growled at me, like an attack dog on a leash.

Tessa raced to my side and helped me up. Her face was white and her eyes round with fear. "Oh my God, Ben! Are you okay?" I groaned, but was able to stand, leaning against her.

The will to fight had left Cory. No one was backing him up. Some threw him disgusted looks and turned away. "Ben," Tessa whispered and yanked on my sleeve. She nodded to the street where a long, black car drove by followed by a procession of other cars.

Everyone fell silent as Luke's family moved past us to the cemetery. One of the kids in the parking lot stood up and waved. A car honked back. A few more kids cheered and the noise picked up momentum. Soon all the kids were standing by the curb waving and cheering and the cars honked back. The noise was deafening.

I closed my eyes and said a silent goodbye to Luke.

TAZ

With tinted windows, the backseat was dim and quiet. Father Johnson sat in front with the driver. Taz could hear his dad's laboured breathing, each inhalation shaking through his ribs. Taz settled into the seat, the leather upholstery newly polished and slippery. Beside him, his mom stared straight ahead, squeezing her hands together in a ball.

"Lots of people showed up," his mom sniffled.

"Yep," his dad looked out the window, his double chin wobbling with emotion.

The car pulled into traffic. Taz wanted to be alone with his thoughts, like he was when he washed windows. But, his mom looked at him, her eyes welling with tears, begging him to break the heavy silence; the way Luke would have.

He started speaking in a low, gravelly voice. "One time when I was about ten, Tyler Featherstone and I were goofing around outside 7-11, trying some wrestling moves we saw on WWE. Luke, came tearing out of Sev, hauls Tyler off me, shouts, 'Leave my brother alone!' and punches him in the nose. Knocked him out! My little eight-year old brother!" Taz grinned, shaking his head at the memory. Tyler had two black eyes for weeks.

His mom cracked a smile. "I never knew that." He was afraid she might start crying again, but instead, a smile stayed on her face. "He always looked up to you. Wanted to do whatever his big brother was doing." Her hands loosened their grip on each other and she smoothed her dress over her knees. One hand lay close to Taz, almost touching his leg. For the second time today, he reached over and held it.

His dad grunted and Taz stiffened, worried that he'd launch into an attack. But he didn't. Instead, his cheek lifted in a half-smile. "The first time he caught a fish, he was about seven, he got so excited, he stood up and tipped the boat over." He shook his head at the memory. "God, there was stuff floating everywhere, the tackle box, rods, paddles. But, Luke never wiped that goddamned smile off his face, even when I was reaming him out for dumping us."

"Do you remember when he was afraid of the tooth fairy?" His mom turned to his dad. "We used to have to go in and check to make sure she wasn't still under the pillow." She gave a soft chuckle. His dad shifted in his seat, moving closer to her.

"He was a good kid."

"Yeah."

"I'm gonna miss him." His dad held a hand up to cover his eyes. Taz watched as silent sobs wracked his body. He'd never seen his dad cry before. His mom rested a hand on his shoulder and leaned against him. The two of them quiet in their misery, but together.

Taz fought his instinct to turn away, pretend he was somewhere else, to keep his emotions hidden from his dad. But, he'd waited for years to see his dad as anything other than an enemy and here it was: his dad laid bare before him, crying and looking for consolation.

Taz stretched an arm across his mom and patted his dad on the shoulder. He let his hand stay there, feeling the bulk of his dad and the stiff fabric of the suit. He froze when his dad reached for his fingers. But, he didn't brush them off. He gripped them, clinging to them as a drowning man might to a rope.

"It's just us now," his dad said and met Taz's eyes.

Us.

Taz's face grew hot as tears of sorrow, relief and exhaustion rolled down his cheeks.

CORY

Cory spat at Ben's heels. The kid didn't even turn around, too busy staring at Luke's hearse. "You're a fucking loser," he said, but his words were drowned out by the other kids' cheers. Fucking morons. It was a funeral procession. They were driving to a grave, not a rock concert. Ben had humiliated him, but he had bigger things to deal with. No gang member bothered with little shits like Ben.

No one noticed when the 'vette peeled out of the parking lot in time to join the end of the line, honking and flashing lights.

When Cory looked in the rearview mirror, it wasn't a seventeen-year old kid that looked back anymore. His cuts had scabbed over, but the sleepless nights and partying of the last week had left hollows in his cheeks. He didn't look like a high school senior. He looked like a gang member. The only thing missing was the grinning skull carved into his chest. But that would come.

He parked by the cemetery and watched as a line of people snaked down the walkway to the gravesite. Images from his father's funeral flashed through his mind; the shiny, honey-coloured wood of the coffin, a dark grain, like a river current, swirling through it. The empty, dark hole dug in a perfect rectangle. The way his mom's body trembled as the coffin was lowered inch by inch. She'd clung to Cory, unable to stand on her own.

He had his hand on the door handle, ready to get out, but he didn't think he could. What if he cried? What if all the feelings he'd kept bottled up for so long came gushing out? In front of everyone. He squeezed his eyes shut.

He needed to get out of here. Yanking the car's gearshift, he reversed and heard the wheels kick stones across the parking lot.

Cory's phone buzzed with a text. It was Michelle. "call me!"

A minute later it buzzed again. "Where r u? call me! It's important"

Probably more of Michelle's drama, but he dialed her cell. He wanted to think about anything other than Luke's coffin being lowered into the bottomless black pit.

"I think Mom's selling Dad's car. She was emailing pictures of it to someone."

"What?"

"I said, I think Mom's selling—"

"Yeah, yeah," Cory said impatiently, "I heard what you said, but I meant, like why?"

Michelle snorted, "Who knows why she does anything these days? She sold his record collection last week to some fat, bald guy with a pinkie ring."

"I wanted those records." Wrenching the wheel, Cory pulled a u-turn without signaling. "She's such a bitch," he spat the words. Michelle didn't say anything.

"Cory? What are going to do?" She sounded worried.

"Teach her a lesson," he said and clicked the phone shut.

The drive to the house gave him time to get angrier. How dare she sell off the only things of his dad's that mattered without asking him? All she cared about was her house, her life, her boyfriend. When he pulled into the driveway, he'd barely put the car in park before he'd pulled the key out of the ignition.

The baseball bat leaned in a corner of the garage. Cory grabbed it, slapping it against his palm. His mom's car was parked in the garage, the windshield replaced. Seeing it freshly washed and undamaged made his blood boil.

The backdoor wasn't locked and Cory barged into the house, his eyes blazing. Straight down the hallway was the front door with its stained glass window. Original to the house, his mom would brag to visitors, as they admired the gemstone colored glass. Cory took a batter's stance and wound up. With one swing, the whole window shattered at his feet, metal spokes hung like icicles from the frame. Next, he swung at the glass sconces, knocking them to the floor and leaving wires dangling from the wall. Moving into the living room, he swung at pictures, the photo of his family on Canada Day, the coffee table, lamps, the TV, a grandfather clock, it all came crashing down in a hailstorm of glass. His mom and Michelle raced into the room, but their screams were drowned out by the noise of Cory's destruction.

With a vicious swing, the dishes and crystal in the dining room cabinet tumbled out the front of it. The antique chandelier came off with a crash and rolled around on the table, crystal teardrops flying around the room. Michelle cowered against her mom in a corner of the staircase, but Cory was oblivious to their fear.

Finally, with sweat dripping down his face and his chest heaving, he let the baseball bat rest at his feet. He surveyed his work with satisfaction.

Glass crunched under his feet. He could hear Michelle choking on sobs and his mom's keening whimper. He dropped the bat, its thud a dull echo of the terror that he'd wreaked upon them. His mom and sister pressed harder against the wall as he approached.

"You were going to sell Dad's car," he explained, desperate for them to understand. "You can't sell it. He wanted me to have it. You can't sell it. You can't sell it." His eyes, wild with exertion, pleaded. Sweat shone on his skin.

"No," she shook her head. Tears had glued strands of blond hair to her face. "No, I'd never!"

"Yes, you would. You were sending pictures. You sold his records. You want to punish me for being there, for not saving him! You blame me for everything. You probably wish that I'd died." Cory yelled like a madman, spit flying out of his mouth.

"That's not true, Cory! You're my son."

Michelle whimpered and clutched their Mom's arm.

"Pictures?" she shook her head as if she didn't understand. "Those were for insurance. After my car got smashed, I got a new policy. The records are in storage, not sold."

Cory gaped at her. Michelle buried her face in her mom's shoulder sobbing in anguish now, not fear. The blood that had pounded in Cory's ears moments before drained from his face.

The wail of sirens grew closer and Cory knew there was no way out.

BEN

When the last car in the funeral procession turned the corner and disappeared everyone moved away from the curb. I stayed where I was, letting everything sink in.

"You did it," Tessa whispered, a triumphant smile crossing her face, but immediately changing to wide-eyed concern. "Are you okay? Do you need to go to the hospital?"

I touched my ribs, and winced. "I feel like I got hit by a truck." Despite the pain, I gave her a dopey-eyed smile.

"Do you kids mind if we go now? I'm not hungry anymore." I'd forgotten about Dad. He'd been standing there, watching Cory hit me and hadn't stepped in. Hadn't done anything to help me. Without waiting for an answer, he started to walk to the car.

"I guess you get your balls from your mom, huh?" Tessa said loud enough for him to hear.

"Guess so," I whispered back.

It hurt to sit, my insides felt swollen. A flap of skin hung loose where Cory had ripped the board out of my hands. Dried blood that had dripped down from my knuckle stained my arm and had smeared across the front of my shirt.

I waited for Dad to say something, ask a question, check if I was okay, but he didn't. When he pulled up to Tessa's house, he got out and held the seat forward for her. She came around to my side of the car as he lit a cigarette on the curb. "You gonna say anything to him?" she asked. "He totally bailed on you."

I was about to shake my head, what was the point? After today, he'd probably disappear for another six months, maybe longer. Tessa shot me a look from the corner of her eye, challenging me.

The smell of his cigarette wafted through the open door. Dad took quick drags and then stubbed it out. Cory wasn't the only person I'd run away from, refusing to stand up for myself. I needed to tell Dad how I really felt.

He shot me a quick, awkward smile as he got back in the car. The longer we drove in silence, the heavier it became. Ask me if I'm okay, I begged in my head. Ask me anything to show you care. Finally, when we were a block from my house, I couldn't take it anymore. A jolt of heat ran up the back of my neck. "You don't give two shits about me, do you?"

His eyes bugged out and he turned to me in surprise. The car behind honked when he crossed a lane of traffic without signaling and pulled to the curb.

Putting the car in park, he pressed his fingers to his forehead. He tried to speak, but his voice broke. Clearing his throat he tried again. "That's not true."

Pent up emotion exploded from me. "You just stood there!" I yelled.

His voice was pleading, high-pitched and whiney. "I didn't know what to do. I just kept thinking what I'd tell your mom if I brought you home all beat up." He leaned back and wiped his eyes with the back of his hand. "I thought I was going to puke every time that kid hit you." He looked out the window and shook his head, "I'm a shitty dad, Ben. I know it, and I know you know it. It's cause of your mom that you turned out so good."

The seat creaked under him as he took a breath and turned back to me. "I'm scared to mess you up." His words sat in the car between us. I stared at him. It was too much, this day. First, Cory and now my dad.

I let the words sink in. It had never been about me not being good enough; it had been about him. He waited for me to say something. "I've spent half my life thinking you don't care about me. That's better?"

"Oh, God, Ben. That's not it."

"Really? Prove it," I challenged him.

He looked at me helplessly. "I don't know how."

"Do anything! Take me for dinner, to a movie, watch me skate." I felt weak with relief, unloading on him had turned my bones to jelly.

He nodded. "Okay."

"No, not just okay. Tell me when. Make plans that you actually keep." It was exhilarating, saying things I'd held back all these years.

"I have Saturday off," he offered. "When's your skateboarding competition?"

"Saturday."

"I'll be there." He grinned.

I didn't share his smile. There was too much history to forgive so quickly. "Don't let me down, Dad."

"I won't." He was about to pull into traffic when he turned to me. "For what it's worth, I was proud of you today. Standing up to that kid took guts."

His words, the ones I'd waited for, were worth more than he knew.

"Hey, Ben," Mom called from the kitchen when I walked in the front door. "Where were you?" She stood in the kitchen doorway drying her hands on a dishtowel. She tilted her head and looked at me suspiciously. "Is that blood on your shirt?" I held up my cut hand.

Shirking off my back pack hurt. I moaned and closed my eyes. Mom pursed her lips, her eyes narrowed. "What happened?"

"After the funeral," I paused. The day's emotional highs and lows started to hit me. I took a deep breath. "Dad took me to the skatepark. To meet the guys from Rox."

She threw the dishtowel against a chair. "You went where?" Her eyes widened in disbelief. She looked like she wanted to rip each hair out of my head, one by one. "After I *told* you not to go!"

"Wait, listen," I said holding up a hand, wincing in pain at the sudden movement. "They want to sponsor me in a competition this weekend. Dad and Tessa were there," I reasoned "Nobody would have tried anything."

"That's not the point. You weren't allowed to go there. I don't care who was with you."

"I know, I know." A wave of pain rolled through my body and I wobbled.

"Ben?" Mom's voice instantly filled with concern.

Gritting my teeth against the soreness in my stomach, I let the rest spill out. "After the skatepark, we went to get something to eat. Cory came up to me in the parking lot." Mom gasped and her hand flew to her mouth.

"Oh God. What did he do to you?" she cried and rushed to me. Her hands trembled as she searched me for injuries.

"I'm okay. He landed a few good ones, but I'm not puking up blood or anything."

She led me to a chair. I collapsed into it, and closed my eyes. The events of the day washed over me. "I stood up to him, Mom. For once, I didn't let anyone push me around. In front of everyone, I called him out."

"What did he do?" she asked.

"Nothing. I had him. And everyone there knew it too."

"And Dad? Where was he in all this? As you were getting beat up?" She started to get angry

I shrugged. "It wasn't his fight. But, we talked, like really talked, in the car. Maybe it'll be different now." I looked at her. The concern on her face melted into something else. Maybe pride? It had only been a week since Luke's fall, but I wasn't the same person I'd been that night. Neither were Taz or Cory. We'd all fallen, flailing our arms and hoping to catch ourselves before we hit bottom.

The gravel still clung to my shoes, but I was walking away.

The End.

Author's Note

Grieving is difficult at any age, but being a teenager complicates the situation. As a junior high teacher, I watched first-hand as the students at my school dealt with the death of a classmate. It was from this experience that the idea for The Fall originated.

    I watched my students experience a life-changing event in different ways. Some of the boys seemed to bottle up their emotions, putting a stopper on expressing their grief, while the girls at my school wept openly and spent lunch hours gathered together in the cafeteria talking about their feelings. Other groups of boys acted nonchalant about their pain, some even reveling in the newfound attention they received since they'd witnessed their friend's death.

    Each of the characters in the book deals with grief in their own way. One finds solace in a gang, looking to lose himself in a different kind of hurt, to punish himself for witnessing not just his friend's death, but another tragic event a few years before. The brother of the victim, turns inward, shutting out his family, even though they are the only ones who can save him as he deals with the guilt of being unable to save his brother. The third character, younger than the others, tries to process what he has witnessed and what it means going forward. Unable to ask for help, he turns to his passion: skateboarding. He ignores the swirling blame surrounding him as he is targeted by classmates for his part in the death of his friend.

While the events I experienced were real and tragic, no part of this book is meant to reflect the students at my school, or their families. It is a work of fiction and should be read as such. I have, however, tried to write as accurately as possible the way young people handle traumatic events.

Acknowledgements

Thank you to Nancy Chappell-Pollack and Gordon Chappell, who read and provided comments on early drafts, and Karen Deeley. I am lucky to have such supportive siblings. Thanks to other enthusiastic readers: Nicholas Cantafio, Laurie Cantafio and Robin Wilson. Thank you also to Genico Aiello, who gave technical advice on the skateboarding sections. Any errors are my own!

Thank you to my husband, Sheldon, who gives me the time and freedom to pursue writing.

Thank you to the staff at Great Plains Teen Fiction, especially my amazing editor, Anita Daher. Her guidance and wisdom have been instrumental in the creation of this book and I am forever grateful.

And, my mom; for letting me believe I could do anything.

An excerpt from Colleen Nelson's

Tori by Design

Available in ebook and traditional format from fine retailers everywhere.

Chapter 1

Part of me wanted to pirouette around the luggage carousel and skip past the bathroom lineup once we landed. But, with the smell of canned air from the plane still clinging to me, a bigger part of me wanted a shower and a comfortable place to lie down. Moving to New York City for a year was my idea, and we were finally here.

Leaving Winnipeg in March, where the streets would be covered with snow for another month and bone-chilling winds blew across the flat prairie landscape, hadn't been hard. But as Mom, my little sister, Ally, and I tried to figure out how to find a cab to take us to the West Village apartment where Dad would be waiting, I wondered if the hard part was just beginning.

A woman verbally attacking someone on the other end of a cell phone nearly flattened me with her roller suitcase. As I apologized, she bulldozed past without looking back. A little stung by her lack of concern, I trailed Mom and Ally to the baggage claim area. Crowds of people jockeyed for the closest position to where the suitcases were spit out, and shoulder checked each other to hoist them off the conveyer belt. No one said excuse me, and as soon as they had their bags, they rushed out of the airport like it was on fire. I started to sweat.

How was my fifteen-and-a-half-year-old self going to navigate around New York City when the airport freaked me out?

As more people grappled with their luggage and hauled it away, another troubling thought popped into my head: What if our bags didn't arrive? This induced more sweating and rapid breathing until all six made their appearance on the conveyer belt, or merry-go-round, as Ally kept calling it.

Limo drivers shouted to Mom asking if we needed a ride, but we dragged ourselves and our suitcases into the line for a taxi. Catching a glimpse of my reflection in the airport windows, I shuddered. It was worse than I thought. A girl with fair skin and a dusting of freckles across her nose stared back at me. My hazel eyes, usually bright, looked sunken and tired after the long flight and weeks of packing. Dark brown hair that normally fell in layered waves around my face had been pulled up into a hasty ponytail, and wispy strands stood out from my head like I'd been electrocuted.

We made it to the front of the line and I stared in wide-eyed amazement as our driver, a swarthy man with furry caterpillars for eyebrows, grunted like a woman in labour and stuffed our bulging suitcases into the trunk of his yellow cab. A bungee cord looped around the yawning trunk was all that ensured nothing fell out. I eyed his knot-tying skills suspiciously, doubting he'd ever been a Boy Scout, and grabbed Mom's arm. "Mom, do you think he cares my suitcases have a year's worth of clothing, shoes and accessories in them?" I whispered. With an exasperated glare, Mom pushed me into the backseat of the cab. It required a contortionist routine to squeeze into the one spot not occupied by carry-on bags or my little sister.

Mom, scrunched up against the door in the front seat, gripped the handle so hard the skin stretched tight and shiny across her knuckles. Every time the driver nearly side-swiped someone in a daring lane change she looked back at us to make sure we hadn't been thrown from the vehicle. I didn't dare ask her if she thought the suitcases were secure.

Ally, oblivious to the sickly sweet vanilla odour of the air freshener, or to the death-race driving, bounced up and down in her seat holding her crusty blanket nicknamed Benkie. She pointed at each building asking if it was the Umpire Steak Building.

"You want the West Side highway or cross-town?" the driver asked Mom. She swivelled in her seat and grimaced at me. Mom's eyes bulge when she's stressed and after a day of airport travel, the driver's question made her look like a Japanese Fighting Fish. Even though we have the same high cheekbones and square chin, with her light hair and blue eyes, we look nothing alike.

Giggling at her expression, I shrugged. "Whichever is faster," I whispered back to her. I was just happy to be out of the airport and anxious to see what sort of apartment we'd be living in for the next year. The photos Dad had sent made it look small and dingy, but he assured us it was just bad lighting.

"Whichever is faster," Mom repeated, trying to sound confident. The taxi driver grunted. Mom winked at me and hunched back into the corner of the black vinyl seat, satisfied with her first response as a New Yorker.

The taxi jerked to a stop a millimetre from the silver BMW ahead of us, and blasted his horn. We were stuck in a traffic jam, and every other driver found it necessary to honk their horn too, as if the noise would magically make the traffic move. I used to get antsy if we were stuck in traffic back home, which was considered heavy if it took longer than fifteen minutes to get anywhere. Cars stretched in front of me for miles. It was definitely going to take longer than fifteen minutes.

Had we really only left Winnipeg that morning? I'd taken one last, lingering look at my room and said goodbye for a year. Every-thing that mattered had been packed up anyway: my sewing machine, clothes, fashion magazines and photos of my friends. Leaving Winnipeg meant giving up everything familiar and comfortable, but the chance to live in New York while my dad taught at a private school for a year was too good to pass up. Especially for me.

I'm a fashion designer.

Okay, I wasn't John Galliano or Stella McCartney—yet—but I did sell my clothes at a funky boutique in Winnipeg called Dresstroyed. All my pieces were made with vintage clothes that I reworked into something new. I'd altered skirts into halter dresses and re-sewed a T-shirt into a miniskirt. My mom taught me to use a sewing machine when I was eight. I used to make clothes from scraps for my Barbie dolls and then I got gutsy and started sewing for myself. The owner of Dresstroyed saw me in his store one day and went crazy for a vest I'd made using one of Dad's blazers from the eighties. When I told him I'd sewn it, he asked if I wanted to sell a few things at his store. Of course, I said "Yes," and started to bring in a few things each week. It was such a thrill the day I walked by his store window and saw one of my dresses on a mannequin.

Nobody is really sure where the design talent came from—my parents haven't worn anything stylish in at least two decades. Half the time they shake their heads at me when I walk out the door to school in my latest ensemble. I'm sure they wonder how a fashionista ended up in their neo-hippie family.

By the time I'd left Winnipeg, the salesgirls at Dresstroyed would fight over who got first pick when I dropped things off. The owner said I had natural talent, but who knows? Designing for Winnipeg girls might be a lot different than designing for New York girls.

Mom and Dad hadn't been completely sold on the idea of moving to New York for Dad's year off work. They'd been thinking about building schools in Costa Rica or living on a houseboat on Lake Ontario. But when I looked online and found a posting for a primary teacher at the prestigious Hayward School in New York City, I practically forced him to apply for it. Ever since I started reading fashion magazines I'd craved the glamour and style of a big city. I came up with reasons to move our family to New York. I'd go to Hayward's Upper School, one of the best high schools in the country; Mom could still work from home as a book editor; Dad would be able to teach, which he loves; and Ally could buy a pretzel as big as her head. Once they saw the genius of my proposal, Dad applied for the job. It took two Skype interviews, but his passion for teaching primary grades won over the Hayward administration and they offered him a job teaching grade two and resource.

The only snag to my plan was leaving my friends. Even knowing I was moving to the fashion capital of the world, saying goodbye had been gut wrenching. Three of my best friends had come to the airport at 6 a.m. to see me off and waited with me until it was time to go through security. We all had red-rimmed eyes and tear-stained faces by the time I gave one final wave from the other side of the metal detector and got ready to board the plane.

A jarring rap on the Plexiglas partition startled me from my reflective state. We were finally moving again. Mom pointed out the windshield. "Look at the Statue of Liberty!" Like one of those rubber bouncy balls, Ally sprang up and down violently in her seat, trying to peer over the dashboard. I finally put a hand on her shoulder to plant her butt on the seat.

"But I wanna see the Statue of Library!" she said, squirming out of my grasp.

"What about shopping, Mom? I need a first day of school outfit." I was semi-whining, but considering the importance of first impressions in a city like New York, I felt it was justified.

Mom shut me up with a look. "I already told you, we'll go shopping. It's only Friday. We have two days before school starts, and you're not the only person in the family, Tori." The warning tone in her voice kept me from saying any more. I sat back in my seat and tried to massage a cramp out of my leg.

Mom's perpetual braid leaked hair after a frazzled day of airports, planes and hauling luggage. Since we'd started planning the move, more grey had appeared in her ashy-blonde hair and the bags under her eyes lingered after her morning cup of coffee. She kept telling me how hard it was to pack up a whole family on her own. Since Dad had left Winnipeg a few weeks earlier to find the apartment and start work, she'd had to arrange everything from forwarding our mail, to renting out our house. There had been some last-minute doctor appointments for Mom and she'd started taking extra vitamins for energy to deal with the move. Over the past few weeks, I'd found the laundry detergent in the fridge and the orange juice in the laundry room.

When we were finally free from the traffic jam—and off the freeway—we found ourselves on a street lined with tidy, red-brick buildings and budding trees, their branches stretching over the cobblestone sidewalk. It didn't look as exotic or fast paced as I thought it would. "Which side?" the taxi driver asked. Mom frantically scanned the block of old brick buildings and shook her head. "The address is 247 Charles Street, but I don't know how far down that is."

"Uh, Mom?" I pointed halfway down the block on her side. Waving in the breeze of passing cars were many, many balloons tied to trees, lamp posts and window grates of a building. As we got closer, I could see a banner over the door that read "Welcome home, Theresa, Tori and Ally!" Mom's excited squeal drowned out my groan of embarrassment.

Ally started to bounce again and would go through the roof if the taxi didn't stop soon. I stayed in the car as Mom leaped out and Ally scrambled to collect her benkie and her pink Barbie carry-on tote. The taxi driver thumped our suitcases down on the sidewalk and waited to be paid.

The front doors of the building burst open and Dad practically jumped over seven cement steps to hug Mom and scoop up Ally, who grabbed him around the neck in a choke hold, her black patent shoes gleaming in the sunlight. With a deep breath, I slid over the black vinyl seat to the curbside door, happily inhaling fresh air.

Dad's wide open arms made me smile. He grinned from ear to ear and I ran into his waiting hug. "Welcome home, Tori."

"I missed you, Dad," I whispered back. He gave me a final squeeze before letting go. Dad lifted Ally onto his shoulders and pulled Mom close and I had to admit, it felt good to have my whole family together again. The four of us stood looking up at the five-storey apartment building that would be our home for the next year.

"Okay, ladies! Your palace awaits. Let's get these suitcases upstairs so you can see your new home." Dad picked up one suitcase in each hand and Mom picked up another, which left mine and two others standing lonely on the sidewalk. I needed two hands to slump it up each step and was just about to hoist my suitcase onto the last step when a voice from below called out.

"Mr. Edwards?" As I turned to see who had spoken, I lost my grip on the handle and the suitcase did somersaults down the steps. The hard, grey case landed with a crack at the bottom, and then exploded.

My yell of "No!" echoed down the street. I scrambled down the steps and stuffed my clothes back into the suitcase. As I bent down to grab my underwear off the pavement, I realized my hands were not the only ones throwing things back into my gaping suitcase.

A deep, smooth voice forced me to look up, "Tori, right? I'm Zak. I go to Hayward too."

Available in ebook and traditional format from fine retailers everywhere.